HEARTWARMING

Her Valentine Cowboy

—

Kit Hawthorne

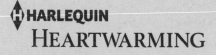

HARLEQUIN®
HEARTWARMING™

ISBN-13: 978-1-335-58483-0

Recycling programs
for this product may
not exist in your area.

Her Valentine Cowboy

For questions and comments about the quality of this book,
please contact us at CustomerService@Harlequin.com.

Harlequin Enterprises ULC
22 Adelaide St. West, 41st Floor
Toronto, Ontario M5H 4E3, Canada
www.Harlequin.com

Printed in U.S.A.

Kit Hawthorne makes her home in south-central Texas on her husband's ancestral farm, where seven generations of his family have lived, worked and loved. When not writing, she can be found reading, drawing, sewing, quilting, reupholstering furniture, playing Irish penny whistle, refinishing old wood, cooking huge amounts of food for the pressure canner, or wrangling various dogs, cats, goats and people.

Books by Kit Hawthorne

Truly Texas

Snowbound with the Rancher
Hill Country Promise
The Texan's Secret Son
Coming Home to Texas
Hill Country Secret

Visit the Author Profile page
at Harlequin.com for more titles.

To all the horse people in my life. You know who you are. Your knowledge, devotion and capacity for hard work inspire me.

Acknowledgments

Many thanks to everyone who answered my questions about horses, tractors, dozers and the rest—my sister Teri James Gillaspie; my daughter Grace; my husband, Greg; fellow authors Nellie Krauss and Janalyn Knight; and local horsewoman and leatherworker Janine Hunt. Thanks also to the members of the Vsetin Czech Moravian Brethren Church, especially pastor's wife Vernell Labaj, who cheerfully and tirelessly answered my many questions about Czexan culture and cuisine and never made me feel like a pest. As always, thanks to my critique partners: Mary Johnson, Cheryl Crouch, David Martin, Janalyn Knight, Willa Blair, Nellie Krauss and Ani Jacob. Special thanks to my reader Monika in New England, who encouraged me to follow up on the taco-kolache place mentioned in some of my earlier books. Thanks also to my editor, Johanna Raisanen, who always makes my books better.

CHAPTER ONE

ROQUE FIDALGO LAY flat on his back on the full-size mattress that made up the sleeping quarters of his live-in horse trailer. The mattress was shoehorned in over the trailer's gooseneck hitch, which put the ceiling about a foot and a half away from his face. Tiny curtainless windows ran down the narrow strips of wall on two sides, but there was nothing to see through the dirty glass except the rusted corrugated metal of the old barn that the trailer was parked inside.

Sometimes in the mornings, if Roque didn't hop right out of bed the minute his alarm went off and start filling Cisco's feed bucket with grain, Cisco would saunter over into the barn and eyeball him through one of the windows. If that didn't work, he'd lean his thousand pounds or so of horseflesh against the side of the trailer and rock it back and forth until Roque finally rolled out of bed.

But Cisco hadn't done that this morning. Maybe he was standing hock-deep in snow out in his sorry excuse for a pasture, too downhearted to even care. Or staring across the road at the huddled buildings of the frozen Texas town, wondering how his life had come to this and what was the point of it all.

Roque eased his body out of his sleeping area, down the ladder and onto the nine square feet of floor space, trying not to bump into the little drop-down table where he kept his electric kettle and French press, but bumping into it anyway. A minifridge and microwave were stacked in the corner between the table and the door. That was the kitchen. There wasn't any stove. As far as food went, if it couldn't be nuked, reconstituted, eaten straight from the package or bought ready-made, Roque didn't eat it.

He could hear the whine of the faucet he'd left streaming into the rust-stained bathroom sink on the other side of the pleated folding door. At least his pipes hadn't frozen.

Lately Roque had been making a lot of these *at least* statements to himself. At least he had his health. At least his truck still ran. At least his bank balance was somewhat above zero. At least he had his horse. He held on to these things like handholds on the side of a cliff.

He rolled his left shoulder a few times, trying to ease the deep ache out of the deltoid and pectoral muscles. Over a year since he'd been hurt, and he still wasn't back to a hundred percent. A couple of 9-millimeter bullets could do that to a guy.

He picked up his jeans from the floor and pulled them on, leaning his hip against the ladder for balance, then stepped into his cowboy boots. His entire living space was smaller than most modern closets— and as a frame carpenter who'd built his share of closets, Roque ought to know. It was all right as a place to crash and keep his clothes, but as a place to hang out for hours on end with nothing to do but think about his life, it sucked.

He'd been snowbound for the past four

days, and stir-crazy didn't even begin to cover it. Power outages had kept the light and heat off more often than not, but he'd wasted precious phone juice watching action movies until the Internet went out completely on the third day, after which he'd just stared at the fake wood grain on the warped ceiling panels, and thought.

And thought.

And thought.

An insulated coffee mug stood on the little triangular corner space above the microwave, next to a tower of empty Styrofoam cup-o-noodle containers and a pair of spurs. Roque picked up the mug and drained the last of yesterday's coffee. It was ice-cold and tasted like diesel fuel.

The cold air outside his trailer door hit him like a slap in the face. There were two trailers parked inside the metal barn—one for living in, and one for hauling Cisco around. The live-in one was of eighties' vintage, solid steel and ridiculously heavy to tow by today's standards. The other, the one Granddad had left him in his will, was newer and lighter, but didn't have living quarters.

The barn's big sliding door stayed open

so Cisco could come and go as he pleased. Most mornings, he was ready and waiting at the back of the live-in trailer, where Roque kept the feed, but not today. Roque opened the loading door and filled the bucket without Cisco whuffling in his ear or nudging him in the back to hurry him along.

He walked out into the pasture—really just a one-acre lot on the edge of town, roughly fenced with scrounged materials.

"Cisco!" he called. "Come and get your breakfast, buddy!"

The gray morning swallowed up the sound of his voice. No answering neigh came back to him, no clop of hooves headed his way.

He walked out past the old slab foundation of the house that had been started decades ago and then abandoned. The edges were all grown up with dried weed stalks and brushy tree limbs tall and thick enough to hide a horse.

He came around the edge, then stopped in his tracks.

The wooden fence post on the corner of the lot had split near the ground, and the wire fencing on either side of it lay flat.

He turned, slowly scanning the lot. Cisco wasn't there.

A wave of nausea rose in his throat. He heard his breath going in and out fast, and saw it making a cloud of fog in front of his face. He shut his eyes and took a deep breath.

"Okay, okay," he muttered. He had to get his head right and figure this thing out.

He opened his eyes. To the north and east of him lay the downtown area of Limestone Springs. Southward were mostly big residential lots like this one, anywhere from one to ten acres in size, but with actual houses on them, not bare slab foundations like on this one. Westward, the land opened up into ranches and farms along Highway 281. The roads were empty now, as they had been for most of the past four days, but that didn't mean Cisco hadn't been hit by an out-of-control vehicle. He could be lying in a bar ditch right now, or on the side of the road, hurt and cold and alone.

Roque walked over to the flattened section of fence. Cisco's tracks were clearly marked in the snow, leading west. But there was no trace of him now.

Roque thought fast. Should he track Cisco

on foot, or take the truck? The roads were still slick, with no salt or sand to provide traction, but at least there weren't any other motorists to crash into him. Yeah, he'd take the truck so he could follow Cisco's tracks while they were still clear. The main thing was to find the horse quickly, before he got hurt. Once Roque did that—he refused to think in terms of *if*—he could find a way to secure him and then come back with his hauling trailer to bring him home.

He hurried back to his living quarters to get his keys, then grabbed a lead rope and halter out of the hauling trailer. Within a few minutes, he was on his way.

The icy roads were eerily empty beneath a chilly gray sky. Swags of snow-topped green garland hung on the front fencing of a neighboring pasture, with jaunty red bows on the posts in between. Somehow the cheery decor made the desolation worse. The whole town looked blank and cold, like a movie set after the filming was done and the actors and film crew had all gone home.

It was the day after Christmas, about three weeks shy of a year since Roque had first driven the eighteen hundred miles or so from Jersey City to Limestone Springs, with nothing but a pickup truck and a headful of dreams, ready to claim his inheritance and become a cowboy. In the months since, he'd had more setbacks than victories, but that hadn't fazed him. He hadn't expected it to be easy, and he liked a challenge—the harder, the better. Being told he couldn't do something only made him want to prove that he could.

That was the attitude that had kept him going the past eleven months. His step-cousin Dirk, his family back in New Jersey and everyone who'd ever given him the stink eye in the feed store—he'd show them all. He had his horse and saddle, his muscles and skills, and the thing inside him that wouldn't quit.

But that was before he'd spent four days trapped in his dismal tin can of a home—over Christmas, no less—with nothing to distract him from the fact that he was alone and underemployed, in a community that didn't want him, with a dwindling bank balance and no prospects for improvement.

And now…

Now even his horse was gone.

He swallowed hard. He loved that big bay horse like a brother. The words of Granddad's last message to him, words of hope in those dark days in that hospital room over a year ago, came drifting up like smoke from a doused fire. *I'm sorry I can't do more for you. I hope it's enough for a fresh start.* As if he'd had a glimpse into the future, and known that a fresh start was exactly what Roque would need. Losing Cisco meant losing that chance, and letting Granddad down.

It felt like a sign. Maybe it was time for Roque to cut his losses. Dirk had made a standing offer to buy back Cisco and the trailer if ever he decided to give up and go home. Maybe Roque ought to take him up on it—for Cisco's sake, if not for his own.

He shook his head hard. No! This was his chance to make something of his life, given to him by the one person who'd still believed in him. He couldn't throw that away.

He had to get Cisco back.

CHAPTER TWO

SUSANA VRBA STARED at the fifty-two buckets stacked in uneven towers on the snowy ground just outside the feed barn. Four days of freezing temperatures, intermittent electricity and isolation had worn her out. She'd been feeding horses, goats, llamas and donkeys, morning and night, all by herself except for Pirko, whose contribution amounted to nothing more than companionship and moral support.

Pirko sat on her haunches at Susana's side, eyeing the buckets with an intelligent gaze. The medium-small dog had a spaniel-like head, with a round forehead and curly floppy ears, and the shape of a border collie, with a trim little waist, light feathering at her legs and a plumy tail. She didn't have the thick border collie undercoat, though, and Susana could see her shivering with cold. Pirko could have stayed inside the relative warmth of the house if she'd wanted, but any time there was work to be done on the place, she was right there in the thick of it.

The weather was supposed to moderate today, but in the meantime, Susana had another feeding to get through, and staring at the buckets wasn't going to get it done.

She picked up a stack of buckets in her gloved hands and opened the doors to the feed barn.

She called it a barn, but it was really just a glorified shed, neatly organized and crammed to full capacity. One wall held a saddle rack and bridle hooks; she referred to that part as the tack room.

The air was marginally warmer in here, with a wholesome oaty scent that always made her think of sunshine. *Grit, grit* went the fine layer of feed crumbles beneath the soles of her work boots as she carried the buckets to the feed bins—big metal trash cans with their lids bungee-corded on to keep rodents out. Above the bins, rough wooden shelving held plastic containers full of wormers, syringes, antibiotics, gauzes and other medical supplies. Up in the loft—really just the highest, deepest shelf—some worn horse blankets formed a lounging area for three cats that were just coming awake, blinking in the thin wintry sunlight. They earned their keep by hunting rodents and snakes, but they weren't too tough for a cuddle.

Susana opened the bins and started scooping. One held regular sweet feed for the horses who were on a maintenance diet; the other held senior feed for those who needed extra calories. Some of the horses got hoof supplement or some other addition to their feed; she color-coded their buckets to keep track. She had the whole thing charted out with a posted list of all the animals' feeding requirements, along with a map of who was penned where and what they all looked like. She didn't really need the chart—she had all the information in her head—but she liked having things documented. And theoretically, if anyone ever fed in her place, they'd need clear written instructions.

Not that she was planning to kick up her heels and go on vacation anytime in the foreseeable future, much less allow herself a sick day. She'd fed every morning and evening for well over two years now. Whenever anyone in her big extended family got married or buried, she had to leave the gathering in time to make it home for evening feeding; whenever she was sleep-deprived or feverish or had a sore throat, she sucked it up and fed anyway. She'd have to be seriously incapacitated to miss a feeding, and just thinking about the possibility of such a thing gave her a panicky, fluttery feeling inside, because what would happen then? She really ought to get a replacement trained up just in case something happened to her, but she didn't have the time or energy to spare to find or train one. It was impossible to move ahead when she was barely hanging on.

She carried the filled buckets to the bed of the feed truck, grabbed some more empties and headed back to the barn.

Two of the cats had jumped down from the loft. Haystack, a longhaired orange tabby, was already munching spilled horse feed from the floor. Chauncy, black-and-white with tuxedo markings, stretched luxuriously, then abruptly froze, snapped to attention as if he'd seen a ghost, and darted outside. Pirko chased him as a matter of form, at a speed just fast enough to look like an earnest effort without any possibility of actually catching him. She came back quickly when Susana told her to.

The third cat, a calico called Ermentrude, was still lolling around in the loft.

"You've got the right idea, Ermentrude," Susana said. "Stay in your warm bed for as long as you can."

Back and forth she went, filling and loading buckets. Pirko kept right by her side, trotting along in her businesslike way as if she were a vital part of the process.

As soon as the last buckets had been filled, Pirko ran to the driver's side door of the truck and waited to be let in. Susana loaded the buckets into the truck bed, then opened the door. Pirko hopped inside and scampered over to the passenger side of the bench seat, where she sat, proud and alert, staring straight ahead.

The various enclosures were separated by T-post fencing, with a lane wide enough for a truck running between the two major sections. Susana drove to the first set of pens, parked, grabbed some buckets out of the truck bed, emptied them into the feeders, broke the ice in the water, returned the empty buckets to the bed and got back in the cab to do it all again. At each stop, Pirko got out and trotted over to the correct pen. She knew the routine perfectly and never made a mistake. If only she could carry buckets, or drive the truck.

The horses came to meet them, tossing their heads and whickering their greetings. Most of them had roommates for companionship—two to a pen, with compatible personalities and dietary requirements— but the crankier ones were on their own.

Some of the horses had to wear blankets, either because they were thin and old, or because their owners just wanted them to. Blankets were a real pain. You had to get them on exactly right, starting with a dry horse if at all possible, then monitor him throughout the day to make sure he wasn't overheating and hadn't wriggled out.

Meriadoc, an elderly Arabian, was an

expert at getting his blanket off. He'd done it at least once a day throughout the snowstorm, and he'd done it again last night. Now he stood beneath the shelter of his open shed, looking innocent and a little sorry for himself, as usual.

"Don't give me that look," Susana told him. "I put that blanket on you and you took it off of your own free will. If you're cold, it's your own fault."

She dragged the blanket out from where he'd contrived to half bury it, shook out the worst of the dirt and snow and heaved it into the bed of the truck.

"There," she said. "I don't have time to get it clean right now. You'll just have to go au naturel."

The worst of the cold weather was supposed to be over by now anyway. The snow hadn't started melting yet, but the parched, sun-bleached grass showed through in some of the higher windswept spots. For the past several months, Seguin County had been going through a drought, with a burn ban leading right up to the snowstorm. Susana had had to buy feed and hay all summer and fall. She yearned for the sight of green grass.

She made the rounds, feeding and breaking water at each pen, and making sure the horses were all in good shape. Daisy, the pregnant palomino mare, looked fit and energetic; she'd come a long way since Susana had rescued her from that horrible place in Schraeder Lake. Domino, a black-and-white paint, was favoring one back leg, but no more than he usually did in cold weather. She checked his hooves just in case, and he gladly seized the opportunity to lean against her to take a load off. Fortunately, he wasn't very big, but neither was Susana.

The last pen held some rescue donkeys, a free-to-a-good-home llama that she'd found on a Facebook group and a miniature goat that someone had dropped off at the local animal shelter in the dead of night. The donkeys' feet had been so overgrown when Susana first brought them home that they'd looked as if they were wearing wooden shoes, the llama's wool had been a dense tangle of mats and the miniature goat had been so thin Susana could count his vertebrae. After months of patient care, they were all healthy and happy.

About two-thirds of the horses on her place belonged to boarders. The rest—and these were generally the more woebegone animals—were hers. She'd bought some at auction, others through private deals. They hadn't cost much, which was how she'd persuaded herself to buy so many. Once rehabilitated, they could be sold to good homes, sort of like flipping houses. That was the theory, at least.

But once the drought had started, and the grass had died, and the rising price of feed had made it prohibitively expensive to keep large animals, she'd been acquiring them faster than she could sell them. She'd eventually sworn off auctions and stopped checking livestock sales online. She couldn't properly care for the animals she already had if she kept bringing home more.

Then people had started *giving* her their unwanted horses.

We just can't afford to keep him anymore, but we know you'll take good care of him. You've got all this land out here, and lots of other horses for company. We'll miss him, but we know he'll be better off with you. That was the gist of what they all said. It didn't seem to occur to them that feed wasn't free for her either or that grass wasn't exactly abundant right now. No one had offered her a surrender fee, and she hadn't had the heart to ask. So her feed bill steadily rose, along with her labor, while her boarding income remained the same, and her bottom line sank.

You can't keep this up, Zuzanka, her mother had said last week when she'd come by to drop off a load of Christmas presents and half a refrigerator's worth of holiday food. *You can't save the world all by yourself.*

But what choice did she have? She couldn't turn away an animal in need. She just couldn't. But her finances and personal energy were strained to the limit. Something had to give.

She finished her feeding circuit back at her starting point and began unloading the empty buckets from the truck bed. The thermometer on the feed barn gave the temperature as thirty-three degrees, which was a lot warmer than yesterday, but not exactly balmy. She hadn't been truly warm in days.

She was just plain worn out. Right now, more than anything, she longed to be taken care of, back in the cozy, comfortable house where she'd grown up, with her big, loud family around her, and her mother to fuss over her. Her parents had wanted her to spend Christmas—and the snowstorm—with them, but of course that had been impossible.

Maybe she'd go inside and take a nice long hot bath with those fancy bath salts her sister Monika had given her for Christmas—but, no, she couldn't, because her pipes had busted during the snowstorm. The outdoor hydrants still worked, because they were powered by windmill and not an electric well pump, so they could keep trickling despite power outages. She ought to feel grateful for that, but all she felt was chilled to the bone, and grungy from wearing unwashed clothes.

Not much like that guy at the feed store the other day—the one the townsfolk called Bobby Six-Guns on account of his over-the-top cowboy getup. Susana smiled at the memory. She'd been hearing about him since last winter, but that afternoon was the first time she'd actually seen him in the flesh.

He'd walked in wearing a knee-length oilskin coat that would have made more sense in the Australian Outback than the American West, along with a black pinch-front felt hat set at a cocky angle, with an eye-catching turkey feather stuck in the braided band. The jeans were right, anyway—boot-cut, dark wash and long enough to wrinkle up at the ankles over his insteps—but too new. His boots were nicer than any Susana had ever owned in her life, with a sharply angled heel, and vamps made of what looked like caiman belly.

A cluster of older men—Roy Davidge, Willis Clark and Gene Harris—stood in their usual spot near the cash register, talking about the upcoming snowstorm and whether it would turn out to be as bad as the weather forecasters said. Now they fell quiet, leaving the hollow thuds of the man's long-spaced footfalls to echo in the silence.

It wasn't that there was anything *wrong* with the guy's clothes, exactly. They'd be fine on a singer in a young country band, making a music video, dancing around in front of old storefronts to the accompaniment of an electric guitar. And the guy certainly had the looks, build and confidence to wear them well. But genuine cowboy fashion, at least around here, tended to be a lot more hit-or-miss. Like cowboy boots with non-boot-cut jeans, the legs all bunched up around the pull straps. Or boots with cargo shorts, or yoga pants. Cowboy hats with T-shirts. Ball caps with button-downs. A hoodie under a Carhartt jacket. Those were the fashion choices made by people who were too busy living the life to bother looking the part. It was a shame, because the old-time authentic cowboy look was a good one. There were a few local guys left who kept up the aesthetic, like Dirk Hager over at the Hager Ranch, but their gear showed honest wear.

Bobby Six-Guns stepped up to the counter. Behind the cash register, Jimmy

Ray Boyd had his mouth twisted to the side like he was trying to keep a laugh from escaping.

"Yessir," he said. "Can I help you?"

"Yeah, I'd like two bags of Alfa Force and a bale of Coastal," said Bobby Six-Guns. He had an unmistakable East Coast accent, and not the South Carolina kind.

Jimmy Ray rang up the order. As Bobby reached into his back pocket, Susana saw that his fancy coat had a saddle gusset with straps on the inside, loosely holding it to his legs. She had to admit, that would be a handy feature for riding, and walking around in high winds.

"That's some coat you got there, mister," said Roy. "You been out riding the range?"

Gene snickered. Jimmy Ray covered his mouth with his hand and cleared his throat.

Bobby froze with his arm bent back, giving Susana a good view of his face, with its expressive dark eyes, close-cropped black beard and big interesting nose. Susana had always been partial to a big nose on a man, as long as the rest of the face was strong enough to pull it off, which Bobby's definitely was. He had the bone structure of a Roman emperor.

"Ooh, better watch out, Roy," said Willis. "He might draw on you."

Gene laughed a little louder this time. Jimmy Ray broke into an unconvincing coughing fit.

Bobby's gaze hardened and his lips compressed. For a second, Susana thought a fight might actually break out, right there in the feed store.

Then something in his expression shifted. He swallowed; she saw his Adam's apple bob. If she had to guess, she'd say his feelings were hurt.

His eyes met hers. And in that moment, everything clicked into place. She *knew* this guy. Well, not in the sense that they'd ever been introduced, but she'd seen him before, years ago—seen him and spoken to him, though never more than a few words at a time. He was the reason she liked big noses on men to begin with. The source of her ideals of manly beauty. She'd never seen him anywhere other than the town's Persimmon Festival, but he'd been a vital part of her young girlhood. All year long, she used to look forward to their next meeting, hoping this would be the year they would exchange more than pastries in a paper bag.

But he'd stopped coming, and she'd never seen him again...until now. Her girlhood crush, that handsome, swaggering boy with the heart-melting smile, had finally come back to town, only to become the town pariah.

She glanced away, embarrassed, as if she'd walked in on him undressing.

He pulled out a fancy tooled-leather wallet and handed Jimmy Ray his debit card. He held his head at a proud angle, with his shoulders back and his chest out, like an animal making a display, like that moment of vulnerability had never happened. But animals had an instinct not to show when they were injured.

Susana swallowed over a painful lump in her own throat. All her protective instincts were roused. Roy and Willis were behaving like a couple of schoolyard bullies, with Gene as their lackey. She longed to march over there and tell them off. But her younger brothers had never appreciated having her stick up for them against other boys, and she had a feeling this guy wouldn't, either.

Jimmy Ray handed him his card and receipt and told him to drive around to get his feed loaded. Jimmy Ray's voice was carefully neutral. No need to offend a paying customer.

Bobby Six-Guns passed by Susana on his way out of the store. The full force of those dark eyes hit her hard. He was even better looking up close. Her heartbeat quickened, and she felt a hint of heat rising to her face.

He tipped his hat to her, like a character in a Western. "Ma'am," he said in his East Coast voice.

Fresh titters rose up before the door had finished swinging shut behind him. It was barely decent, the way these guys were acting.

"Hoo boy," said Roy. "Can you believe that guy? Who does he think he is?"

Gene shook his head, still staring at the door. "Talk about your dime-store cowboys."

Roy made a scoffing sound. "Drugstore, Gene. The term is drugstore cowboy, not dime-store. He doesn't hang out at the Dollar General."

"Well, he doesn't hang out at Walgreens, either," Gene shot back.

"He must be one of them new folks out at Masterson Acres," said Willis.

Masterson Acres was a new subdivision of twenty-acre lots carved out of an old family ranch, and the source of a whole minefield of hard feelings in town.

"Cain't be," said Jimmy Ray. "The Masterson land wasn't even sold when that bozo first showed up."

"Maybe he's a drifter," said Willis. "The Man with No Name."

Gene guffawed at that.

Susana took her selections—several twelve-packs of ivermectin and a tub of glucosamine—to the counter. "You all think you're so hilarious, don't you? Mocking him to his face. You ought to be ashamed of yourselves."

Roy gave her a squint-eyed glare. "Don't waste your pity on the likes of him, missy," he said. "It's guys like him who keep coming in from out of state, buying up property and driving up the price of acreage, and making it next to impossible for honest folks who've lived here all their lives to afford land of their own."

"You don't know that," Susana said. "You don't even know his name."

"I know all I need to know. Anyone who can afford to buy cowboy clothes that look like they came straight off a movie set, and has the nerve to put 'em on and prance around the feed store in 'em, clearly has more money than sense. Whoever he is, and wherever he came from, he doesn't belong here."

Susana hadn't had an answer for that, and she'd done her best to put Bobby Six-Guns out of her mind. Now, with morning feeding done and a day's worth of work ahead of her, she did it again. She already had plenty of needy creatures to look after without worrying about a stray wannabe cowboy.

CHAPTER THREE

SUSANA STACKED THE last of the buckets
by the feed barn, where they'd be waiting when she came back in eight hours to
do it all over again. She straightened and
stretched, trying to ease the soreness out
of her back. A hot bath wasn't an option,
but maybe she could curl up under a warm
blanket with a heating pad—assuming the
power stayed on.

As she made her way toward the house,
a movement at the end of the driveway
caught her eye.

It was a horse.

She stopped in her tracks. What the
heck? What was a *horse* doing ambling
up her driveway all by himself? Had one
of the boarders escaped? None of them
had been missing at morning feeding. Had
her fencing come down along the road at

some point in the past few minutes since she'd finished her circuit?

She turned and scanned the pastures, doing a quick head count. No one was missing.

The horse was closer now, coming confidently up the drive. He was a big bay with three white feet and an irregular blaze on his face. None of Susana's boarders or her own horses had that particular combination of markings. This guy was a newcomer.

Well, of all the... Was *this* what it had come to? Were people actually dumping their unwanted horses on her very doorstep now, the way they dumped unwanted cats and dogs in the country? Seriously?

She let out a heavy sigh, then headed over to the horse. Pirko began to follow, trotting importantly along.

"Stay," Susana said, holding her hand, palm out, toward the dog.

Pirko looked a little hurt, but she stopped in her tracks and plunked her hindquarters down.

Susana feared the worst as she drew near. During a drought, when the price of feed skyrocketed, sometimes people just stopped feeding. She'd seen some grim cases over the past several months.

But the bay held his head at a comfortable angle, and his eyes were bright and clear. He was lean but not skinny, with a good amount of muscular flesh covering his bones, and he certainly wasn't fearful. When he saw Susana coming, he stopped, but didn't shy or run, and stood his ground as she closed the distance between them.

He was a gelding, with a definite Quarter Horse look to him. His winter coat was thick and woolly, but reasonably clean, as if he'd been pastured but regularly groomed. His feet could use a trim, but they weren't in bad shape, and the bridle path through his mane was neatly clipped.

He wasn't starved or otherwise neglected, and unless Susana missed her guess, he wasn't abused. All of which made it far less likely that he'd been abandoned.

So what was he doing here?

She reached out a hand and laid it on his neck. "Where'd you come from, huh, bud?"

He wasn't wearing a halter. Susana cupped one hand behind his jawbone, placed the other on the bridge of his nose and led him toward the covered arena. He came willingly enough. Pirko watched, still sitting where Susana had left her. As soon as Susana reached the gate, though, the little dog couldn't restrain herself any longer. She circled around behind the horse and followed him in, as if herding him through. The horse ignored her.

Susana shut the gate and stood studying him. Some of her near neighbors had horses, but she knew all those animals by sight. Maybe someone had just bought a new one and he hadn't quite settled in.

And yet… Wasn't there something familiar about him? Something niggled at the back of her memory, saying she ought to recognize this horse.

She took out her phone and pulled up the group text she had going with all the property owners within five miles or so. This was where they let each other know that someone had a cow out, or a new stray dog had been spotted in someone's pasture, or someone's horse shed had gotten blown down, or whatever.

She typed, Anyone lose a big bay gelding? I just had one show up at my place. I'll keep him in my arena until I hear back.

In the meantime, she might as well do some groundwork with the horse. He had nice manners, and she was curious about his training.

The group text replies came back quickly as she was gathering tools—a Clinton Anderson knotted rope halter, a fifteen-foot lead rope and a whip. No one had lost the horse or knew where he'd come from.

The horse responded well to groundwork, longeing, stopping and backing on command. Pirko watched from her spot near the fence, her intelligent eyes following the horse's every move. Wherever he came from, someone had taught him well.

How could such a valuable animal just wander off unnoticed?

Suddenly, his head lifted high, his ears pricked forward, and he let out a loud neigh. Susana followed his gaze. A beat-up truck was ooching down the road toward her place.

It had been days since Susana had seen any motor vehicle other than her own. Texas roads rarely got icy, and when they did, it was best to stay home. But this truck was creeping along at a safely slow speed—and the bay knew the sound of its engine.

Susana slipped through the bars of the arena fence as the truck turned into her driveway and parked near the house. The driver's side door opened, and a man stepped out—a tall broad-shouldered man in an oilskin drover coat, wearing a black felt cowboy hat with a turkey feather in the band. A man with the profile of a Roman emperor.

Bobby Six-Guns.

He was scanning the area; he hadn't seen Susana yet. In a carrying voice with a distinctive northeastern accent, he called out, "Hello! Is anyone home?"

The bay whinnied again, and Susana replied, "Over here."

The man turned. Even from this distance, she could see the flash of white teeth in his face as he caught sight of the horse in the arena. He hurried over, still grinning, down the packed track left by the feed truck.

The bay met him eagerly at the fence, giving him a friendly whuffle. The man reached for the animal, circling the coppery neck with his arms.

"Cisco! You bad horse. What's the big idea, running off like that, huh? You want I should worry to death?"

Cisco! Of course. This was Henry Hager's horse that he used to ride on his ranch. What was he doing with Bobby Six-Guns? Had Dirk sold Cisco after his grandfather's death? That didn't seem like something he would do.

Cisco nuzzled the man in the shoulder. Bobby Six-Guns rested his forehead against the horse's, shut his eyes and let out a sigh.

Then he turned to Susana, his smile lighting his face again—the smile she remembered from all those years ago. The boy from the Persimmon Festival, her romantic ideal, was actually here on her property.

"Thanks for looking after my boy, here," he said. "When I went out this morning and he wasn't there—" He shook his head and shuddered. "Well, it was a bad moment, I can tell you that. I was able to track him for a while, but I lost his trail. I've been driving around and around, just hoping to catch sight of him. I'm so glad he's okay."

Susana started to ask why he hadn't just called or texted his neighbors. That's what she would have done if a horse of hers had wandered off. Then she realized he probably wasn't on speaking terms with any of them.

"You're very welcome," she said. "How did he get out?"

"One of my fence posts split. An old wooden one. Looks like it had a crack in it that filled up with sleet, and it broke right off."

"That would do it, all right. Where's your place?"

"Corner of Persimmon and 281."

She thought about that. "Isn't that the lot the Mendozas own, out on the edge of town?"

"Yeah, that's right. Mr. Mendoza's been renting it to me."

She couldn't be understanding him properly. "And...you're saying you pasture your horse there?"

"Yep." He gave her a wry smile. "I know what you're thinking. It's not a great place to keep a horse, but it's all I can afford right now."

"Where do you live?"

"Same place."

"The Mendozas' lot? I didn't think there was a house on the property." Not a finished one, at least. Nothing but a decades-old foundation for a house that had never been built.

"There's not," he said. "I've been staying in Mr. Mendoza's old horse trailer from when he used to do rodeo."

She stared. "That old behemoth from the eighties?"

"That's the one. It may look big on the outside, but most of it is horse stalls and tack room. The living quarters are microscopic."

"But...but what did you do during the snowstorm?"

He laughed. "Froze my butt off. But so did most everyone else, I guess. I'd like to get me some acreage, build a little house, but…well…it hasn't happened yet."

Susana didn't know what to say. Everyone, herself included, had been assuming Bobby Six-Guns was a rich eccentric. Looked like they were wrong.

"I'm Roque, by the way," he said. "Roque Fidalgo."

Susana extended her hand. "Susana Vrba," she said.

He had a good handshake, firm but not overpowering. "Good to put a name to the face at last," he said. "We've met before. Well, not met exactly, but seen each other."

Her heart seized up, her mind went blank, and all she could say was, "Um?"

"At the feed store," he said.

Right. The feed store. As far as he knew, that was the first time he'd ever laid eyes on her. The little girl at the kolache stand obviously hadn't made as big an impression on him as he had on her. Story of her life.

"The feed store," she repeated. "Yes. I remember."

Her cheeks grew warm, and she glanced away.

Roque misunderstood her awkwardness. "It's all right," he said. "I know I'm not the most popular guy in town."

Pirko was circling Roque's feet by now, waggling and whining, beside herself with joy at having a visitor. He stooped down to pet her.

"Hey, there," he said to the dog. "And what's your name?"

"That's Pirko," said Susana.

Roque's voice went all sweet and goofy. "Pirko! What a pretty name for a pretty dog."

"It means feather in Czech," Susana said.

"Very appropriate," said Roque. He rubbed Pirko's ears and under her chin. Pirko put her paws on his shoulder and laid her head against his chest.

"I'm sorry," Susana said. "She's a very affectionate dog. Always has been—for as long as I've known her, at least."

"How long is that?" asked Roque.

"About a year and a half. She just showed up one day. No collar or chip, and her coat was dry and dull like she'd been undernourished. None of that put a damper on her pluck, though. She went right to work with me like she was born to it."

Roque looked indignant. "Man. What's wrong with people? Why would anyone abandon a terrific little dog like this?"

As if she knew what he was saying, Pirko licked Roque's chin and nuzzled his neck. She wriggled with all her might, as if trying to work her way as close to him as possible. Susana was embarrassed for her. The dog had no sense of her own dignity. When she liked someone, she was all in.

"Where are you from, Roque?" Susana asked.

He gave Susana a look of mock surprise. "What makes you think I'm not a born and bred Texan?"

It wasn't a serious question, so she didn't answer it, just smiled and waited.

Roque gave Pirko a final pat, stood upright and said, "I'm from New Jersey."

No surprise there. She'd figured either New Jersey or New York. His accent was the kind she associated with mobsters in old movies, which no doubt was a hateful stereotype, but there it was.

Then the million-dollar question.

"So how'd you end up here in Seguin County?" she asked.

He laughed again, but this laugh had a bitter sound to it. "That's a long story," he said.

She thought fast. It was too cold to stand around outside talking, but she was curious about this stranger from the North—curious enough to take a risk. When was she going to have a better chance to find out all about her girlhood crush?

"I'm going to make some coffee," she said. "Would you like to come in and have a cup?"

Something around his eyes softened. All of a sudden, he looked very young, like the boy she remembered.

"Thanks, Susana," he said. "I'd like that a lot."

CHAPTER FOUR

"I LOVE YOUR PLACE," Roque said.

He was sitting at a battered wooden table inside an eat-in kitchen, with a tiny living room behind him, just big enough for a sofa and one armchair. From the outside, the building had looked like a metal barn, which at first glance was exactly what he'd thought it was. But once he'd gotten up close, he'd seen the front porch, with old-fashioned wrought iron chairs pulled up to a cable-reel table that looked like a giant wooden spool, and a red front door with a Christmas wreath hanging on it. The inside was all fitted out and furnished, with lots of homey touches—red-and-white-striped dish towels, crisp white curtains at the windows and even a miniature Christmas tree standing in the corner of the L-shaped kitchen countertops.

Roque drank in the sight like he was

dying of thirst. It had been so long since he'd been inside an actual house. Everything was so cozy and comfortable. Even the dog, Pirko, had her own bright floral cushion by the front door. She was curled up there now, eyeing them both with an alert, intelligent gaze.

Susana filled the electric kettle with water from a pitcher beside the sink. She had half a dozen pitchers lined up on the counter, probably stockpiled for the snowstorm. "Thanks," she said. "It's not much, but it's enough for me."

"Well, compared to where I've been staying, it's a palace," said Roque. "It's so good to be able to sit down and stretch my legs out, and not see all of it at once. Makes me feel restful inside, just knowing there are other rooms behind those walls."

She pressed the switch for the kettle. "It seemed like a lot of space to me, too, at first—but then I'd spent most of my life before that sharing a bedroom with two younger sisters."

"You built the place yourself, then?"

"Not me personally, no. My cousin is in construction. He came out with my dad and brothers and did the work. Saved me a lot of money. A barndominium is a pretty good value to begin with, housing-wise. Low on curb appeal, and inexpensive to build, but fully plumbed out and wired."

Roque nodded. Maybe he could swing a barndominium for himself one day, if he ever managed to get some land to put one on.

"How many square feet you got here?" he asked.

"Seven sixty."

"That all? It looks bigger from the outside."

"Yeah, the other half of the building is a combination garage and storage area. It runs the whole length of the house, right on the other side of the kitchen wall."

"Easy to add on to one day, then. You'd double your square footage without changing the footprint."

"That's the idea—if it ever gets to that point."

Seven hundred and sixty square feet was pretty small for a house, but Susana herself was small—like *really* small. Maybe not even five feet tall. It seemed strange for someone so tiny to take care of horses, but she had a look of strength about her in spite of her size. All her movements were neat and precise, with no wasted motion, like she knew exactly what she was doing. It was a pleasure to watch her walking around her kitchen, spooning coffee grounds into the French press and taking down two sturdy Christmas mugs from the cabinet. She had a fantastic head of hair, thick and glossy, pulled back in a dark brown braid down her back. The braid was as big around as her wrist.

"So is it just you out here?" he asked. "No husband or kids?"

Her hand froze halfway to the coffee canister. He couldn't see her face, but he knew he'd said the wrong thing. There was a different tone in her voice as she said, "Mmm-hmm. Just me."

Roque held his hands up, palms out. "I'm sorry. I didn't mean that the way it sounded. I'm not trying to come on to you or anything, honest. Not that I don't find you attractive! It's just—well, the last thing I need in my life right now is a romantic relationship. I mean, it's one thing to live on ramen noodles and sleep in a horse trailer when it's just me. It's an adventure, you know? But if there was anyone else involved, it would just be sad."

She put the coffee canister away and turned to face him. He could almost see the wheels turning in her head as she sized him up and deciphered his word salad.

"I get it," she said at last. "I'm in the exact same boat—or rather, I'm in a similar boat, by myself. I just wish I could make my mother understand—and my father, and aunts, and grandparents. By the time my mom was my age, she was married with two kids and another on the way. And here I am, no husband, no boyfriend, and no time for dating, even if I wanted to. Every time I visit, it's *So, Zuzanka, is there a young man in your life yet? No? Better get busy, siska. You won't be twenty-seven forever.* They all interrogate me separately, and there are so *many* of them, which means I have to go through the whole thing over and over. It feels like it's all we ever talk about."

"You ought to make a general announcement at the start of every family gathering," said Roque. "Get up in front of the whole group and say, *Yo, listen up! This is me letting everybody know that, yes, I'm still single and, no, I'm not looking to change that. So none of youse needs to set me up with your neighbor's nephew's friend or the nice young man at the butcher shop. Capisce?*"

Susana laughed. "I should, but I don't think I'd have the nerve. Is that what you do?"

He waved a dismissive hand. "Oh, my family gave up trying to set me up years ago. Either that or they ran out of prospects. They kept up the lectures for a while, though. *It's high time you stopped moving across the country from job to job and settled down with a good woman, Roquito.* Now they don't even do that. I guess they decided I'm a hopeless case."

She pulled out the other chair and sat down, tucking one leg underneath her like a child, giving herself some extra height at the table. "See, with me it's the other way around, because I never travel. I can't. I have to feed livestock twice a day, and give lessons, and take care of the animals. Apparently men aren't interested in a woman who's tied to home the way I am, and whose idea of dressing up is putting on a clean pair of jeans. But this is the life I chose. I love what I do. I *love* it."

She said the last sentence fiercely, like he was one of her relatives that she had to convince.

"I feel you, sister," he said. "You're preaching to the choir, here."

The switch popped up on the electric kettle. Susana went over to it, poured the steaming water into the French press and set the lid on top with her small capable hands.

"So how many brothers and sisters you got?" Roque asked.

"Five brothers, two sisters. I'm the oldest of eight."

He tapped his chest. "Youngest of seven, right here."

"The baby of the family, huh? I guess that takes the pressure off you to produce grandchildren, anyway."

"Ha! You'd think so, but no, not really." He picked up a Saint Nicholas sort of figurine and started fiddling with it. "How about you? Any of your younger sibs married or have kids yet?"

She sat back down, folding her leg under her again. "Nope. And if they're waiting for me to set an example, they're going to be waiting a long time."

"So what is it that you do, exactly?" Roque asked. "For work, I mean. Something with horses, obviously. Do you breed them?"

She laughed. "Oh, gosh, no. That's a whole other level in the horse world, and one I don't aspire to. This is a horse-boarding outfit—or *equestrian center*, I should say. I do boarding, riding lessons and trail rides—or I would, if I could ever get the trails constructed. But that's the plan, anyway."

"This is your place, then? You're the owner?"

"Owner, proprietor and sole employee."

He leaned back in his chair and eyed her with fresh respect. "Whoa. That's fantastic! You're really living the dream, aren't you?"

"Absolutely." Her smile faltered. "Mostly. Sort of. I mean—" She sighed. "See, this is what I've dreamed of and worked for all my life. I always said I didn't care about money as long as I could work for myself doing what I love. But I guess I thought there'd be a *little* more money. Enough to hire some help, or pay for the improvements I'd need to bring in additional income."

She traced the wood grain of the table-top with her finger. "Part of the problem is the drought. It's raised my expenses for feed and hay, and brought a whole lot of rescue horses my way. Theoretically, they can be rehabilitated and sold to good homes, but that takes time and effort, and medicine and feed. And in the meantime, that's pasture space that isn't bringing in income from a paying boarder. But what can I do? There are so many neglected horses out there. A lot of people don't re-alize what a big commitment it is, owning a horse, and they bite off more than they can chew. Horses live a long time and need a lot of care, and when money gets tight and schedules fill up, they get abandoned. And that's where I come in."

"Wow, that's…" He searched for a word. "That's heroic."

She shrugged that off. "The way I look at it, it's a duty. People have been living and working with horses for thousands of years. They're a part of us, and we're a part of them. Throughout history, we've used them for agriculture, hunting, transportation, sport, companionship, war. We've bred and trained them to do those things. We've actually shaped the species through selective breeding. And that makes us responsible for them. We don't get to just return them to the wild when we're through with them, or when they get too sick or expensive or inconvenient to keep."

He liked the way she said it. Not dramatic or grandiose, but quiet and matter-of-fact, like this was just an everyday job that had to be done. There was a core of steel inside that tiny body.

"But people do give them up," he said. "And you take up the slack. That's honorable work."

She smiled. "But not very lucrative, unfortunately. You know what they say. Horses eat money. And the work never ends."

"Yeah." He rubbed his chin. "Does it ever get to you? Day after day, the same routine, all that pressure?"

"It didn't used to, but lately, yeah, it does. I keep finding myself daydreaming about town jobs. The kind where you shower before going there, instead of after you get home. Where you dress up, and do your hair, and sit in a climate-controlled office all day, and get weekends and holidays off, and go out to lunch with co-workers who have something to say back to you when you talk to them, instead of just eating grass and then barfing it up on the rug."

Pirko came bounding over, stood up on her hind legs and put her front paws in Susana's lap. Roque let out a snort of laughter.

"Look at that!" he said. "You didn't even say her name, but she knew you were talking about her. She's like, *Yeah, I did that. I barfed on the rug. That was me.*"

"It's nothing to be proud of, Pirko!" Susana said. Then she chuckled. "She's pretty smart, all right, even if she doesn't always put her brains to the best use." She bent down to give the dog a cuddle. "Aw, I didn't mean it, Pirko. You might not be the best conversationalist in the world, or have the best personal hygiene habits, but you sure give the job your all, and you never gossip or play office politics. You're the best coworker I could ask for."

Pirko licked her in the face. Susana laughed, her gloom apparently all gone.

"And you're right," she said to Roque. "I *am* living the dream. Right now I'm tired and discouraged, but I'll get over it. I don't want an office job. Not really. I don't want to put on mascara and heels every day. This is what I love, and I'm going to make it work."

"There you go!" said Roque. "That's the spirit!"

He reached over and gave Pirko a rub on the head. His fingers grazed Susana's. The slight touch sent a sort of tingle through him. Her eyes met his, and her lips curved up in a shy little smile.

Just then, her phone started to buzz, startling them both. She picked it up, dropped it, picked it up again and looked at the screen.

"Sorry, I need to take this," she said.

She flipped her long braid over her shoulder and put the phone to her ear. "Hi. Thanks for calling me back."

Then her face fell. "*How* long?… Oh… No, I understand… Yeah, go ahead and put me on your schedule, then. If I find someone else who's able to come out sooner, I'll let you know. Thanks."

She ended the call and frowned at the screen.

"That sounded disappointing," said Roque.

"Yeah, it was a plumber. The pipes in my house froze up during the snowstorm, and so did everyone else's, apparently. He doesn't think he'll be able to get to me until next week at the earliest." She let out a sigh that puffed her cheeks, then said, "Oh well. I've made it this long. I can hold out another week."

She gave Pirko a final pat, then went over to the French press and pressed the plunger down.

"So how many acres you got out here?" Roque asked.

"Three hundred and eighty-five."

"Three hundred and eighty-five! I don't know a lot about horse-boarding, lesson-giving, trail-riding outfits, but that seems like a lot."

Susana poured the coffee and carried the mugs to the table. "Oh, it's plenty big for the kind of business I want to do, but most of it isn't usable yet. I need to clear the brush, and do some grading, and put up some more fencing, and plan and construct the trails. I really need a proper barn, too, with a feed room and a tack room and lots of stalls. But all that takes labor I don't have time for, and materials I can't afford, at least until my income exceeds my outgo. I could increase that income if I made those changes, but—well, you see the problem."

"Yeah, I get it. So how long you been in business?"

"Two years. I got a good deal on my property because it was a foreclosure and I made a big down payment."

"How'd you manage that at your age?"

"Worked hard and saved my money," she said. "I've always worked, from the time I was a kid. My extended family has a whole lot of restaurants, pastry shops and taco stands between them, and there was always a relative needing help on weekends or summer vacation—you know how it is in a big family."

"I know about the working part, all right," he said. "Not so much about the saving money part. I always blew through my earnings pretty quick."

"Well, I put mine in the bank. I started out saving for a horse of my own, to keep at my grandparents' place. But by the time I had enough, I knew that what I really needed was my own land, and the skills to make a living on it. After high school, I went to a horsemanship academy for seven weeks of intensive study. Once I was certified, I started giving lessons, and training horses, and working on various ranches in the area, and saving money again. So when this place came on the market, I was ready."

Roque shook his head slowly and let out his breath. Setting a big goal, and pursuing it day after day, month after month, year after year—he couldn't even imagine the patience and self-discipline that would take. He got restless if he had the same thing for breakfast three days in a row.

"That's impressive," he said.

"Well, having to wait was good for me, because there was so much to learn," Susana said. "The time I spent working on other people's outfits was invaluable. I didn't have a horse of my own, but I got to work with other people's horses, and I gained experience, and made contacts, and stayed in the loop about properties coming up for sale in the area. I got to see a lot of different layouts and figure out what sort of land I wanted for myself, and how much of it, and how to set it up. After I bought the place, I went right to work, clearing enough brush to set up the pastures I have now, and getting the house built. I put the word out that I was taking boarders, and had a dozen clients lined up before I'd finished the fencing. Most of my pens were full by the end of the first month."

Roque shook his head again. Just thinking about that level of persistence and organization made his head swim.

"So how about you?" Susana asked.

"How about me what?" he asked. He

sure didn't have an inspiring story like hers to share.

She shrugged. "How long have you been riding?"

"Since I was ten. My granddad taught me."

"Did he own land up north?" Susana asked.

"Oh, no, he was a rancher and a lifelong Texan. Had a place not far from here."

"Really? What was his name?"

"Henry Hager."

Susana sat up straight. "Henry Hager! Henry Hager was your grandfather?"

"Step-grandfather, actually. Married to my grandmother. Second marriage for both. But he told me to call him Granddad, and I did. You knew him?"

"Of course! He was one of the ranchers I worked for after finishing horsemanship school. Such a great guy. One of the real old-time cowboys. I was sorry to hear he died."

Roque stared into his coffee. "Yeah, so was I."

"Henry Hager was your step-grandfather," Susana said again. She seemed really struck by this. "That would make Ava Hager your step-cousin."

Roque smiled. "Yeah, that's right. Little Ava. She's a sweetheart. She used to get so excited when Cousin Rocky would come to visit—that's what she called me. My nonna took her to New York City a few times to see the sights."

"I remember that!" said Susana. "I remember Ava going to New York City."

"You knew her, huh?"

"Only a little. She was a few years behind me in school. I never realized…"

"Never realized what?"

"Oh, nothing. It's just funny to think of us knowing some of the same people."

"Yeah, I guess so. Who knows? We might have run into each other as kids at some point."

"Mmm, yeah!" Susana said. "Wouldn't that be something?"

"I loved coming to Texas," said Roque. "I was kind of a hyperactive kid. My nonna brought me to the ranch that first year to give my parents a break. I don't think anyone expected me to take to it the way I did. It was like my head cleared and

I could focus. The land, the animals, the machinery—there was so much going on, but it was peaceful, too. Granddad never lost patience with me, and he could get me to obey without even raising his voice. He was always doing something with me, taking me fishing at the stock tank, teaching me to ride and rope, taking me to cattle auctions. I ate it up."

"So why'd you stop coming?"

He looked at her. "How did you know I stopped coming?"

"Oh, um, didn't you just say so?"

Roque frowned. "Did I? Huh. Well, my nonna died, and she was the one who used to pay my airfare. Granddad said I could still come visit him, but by then, I was fifteen, big enough to be useful on my dad's construction crew, and he didn't think much of losing my labor for three weeks every summer, much less coughing up the cash for the plane tickets. So that was the end of that. I did stay in touch with Granddad over the years—Christmas cards, phone calls. I checked in with him whenever I changed jobs or moved, which was a lot. We used to talk about me coming back to Texas to see him one day, but it never happened. I wish…" He trailed off. "Anyway, that was it, until I got shot."

CHAPTER FIVE

SUSANA STARED. She wasn't sure if she'd heard him properly. "You got shot? Who shot you?"

"Just some guy. Could have been a gang initiation, but they never caught the guy, so I don't know. Maybe he didn't like my face. Maybe he didn't like Mazdas."

"Mazdas?"

"Yeah, I was in my CX-9 at the time. I'd just pulled up at an intersection when the passenger in the next car shot me. Between the gunshot wounds and the resulting car wreck, I ended up with a broken jaw, collapsed lung, shattered tibia, dislocated shoulder, Grade Three concussion, yada yada."

"How awful."

"Yeah. So there I was, stuck in a hospital bed with my jaws wired shut and my leg in traction, on a liquid diet, doped up on painkillers, unable to move or talk or even watch TV. Nothing to do but think. It was the closest I ever came in my life to being depressed."

"I would imagine so," Susana said. Being hurt, unable to speak and confined to bed would be rough on anyone, but for a strong, energetic, talkative, outgoing guy like Roque, it must have been torture.

He ran a hand through his curls. "I was in a bad headspace to begin with. My girlfriend had just left me for another guy. I was frustrated with my job, my apartment, everything."

He glanced over at her, his head still lowered, his eyebrows pushing up some wrinkles in the center of his forehead. "You know what kept me going? The ranch. All those weeks in the hospital, through the pain and the drug fog, made me realize those were the happiest days of my life—riding fence with Granddad, roping cattle, fishing in the stock tank. I wanted to see the stars at night, and hear the wild turkeys gobbling and the coyotes howling. I wanted to ride a horse again. So I said to myself that as soon as I was on my feet, I would go to Texas and see Granddad, and figure out what to do with the rest of my life."

He shifted in his seat.

"The day they unwired my jaw," he said, "I got a call from Granddad's lawyer in Limestone Springs. Granddad was gone. He'd left me a horse, some tack, a horse trailer and some cash. He said he was sorry he couldn't do more for me, but he had Dirk and Ava to provide for, too, and no way was he breaking up the land. As if I had any right to expect anything from him at all! He knew how I'd gone from job to job, how I couldn't seem to stick with anything long enough to settle down. He said it was time to cowboy up."

He took a swallow of coffee. "Well, it was like a sign, you know? So I finished my physical therapy, bought a truck and headed south."

Susana blinked. "Headed south? You mean—you just started driving? To Texas?"

"Sure. I'd made my decision. Why wait?"

He said it like it was the most natural thing in the world.

"Did you have any plans for when you got here? A job? A place to stay?"

He waved a hand. "I don't like to plan things out too far in advance. I'd rather figure it out as I go along. Planning takes away half the fun."

Susana sat back, stunned, thinking of all the hours of research she'd done, pages of notes she'd taken, lists and calendars and spreadsheets she'd drawn up before closing on the purchase of her property.

"Planning *is* half the fun," she said.

"Not for me," said Roque. "Anyway, I figured my step-cousin Dirk would offer me a job. With Granddad gone, he'd need help on the ranch, and who better than me?"

"I'm guessing he didn't see it that way," said Susana.

"You guessed right. He said he was low on funds at the moment and not hiring."

That wasn't surprising. Dirk was a good guy, but probably not thrilled to have his grandfather give away a good horse and trailer, much less a substantial chunk of cash. *Of course* Dirk was low on funds. He'd just had to write a big check to

Roque. Plus it was a fair guess that his loudmouthed Yankee step-cousin had never been his favorite person to begin with. And for Roque to show up unannounced, ready to claim his inheritance, and expecting a job in the bargain, would have seemed the height of arrogance and presumption.

"It was a setback," Roque went on. "But I figured I'd just get a job somewhere else. I know how to ride and rope, I'm strong, I learn quick and I'm not afraid of hard work. So I went to the feed store and asked if anybody was hiring cowboys."

"You did *what*?" Susana asked.

"Asked for a job at the feed store. Said I needed some cowboy work to tide me over until I was ready to buy my own place."

Susana cringed inwardly. She could picture the scene. A stranger with a northern accent, probably clothed head to toe in brand-new over-the-top Western wear, bragging about his riding and roping skills, making noise about buying land—everything about it was offensive.

"What did they say?" she asked, though she pretty much knew the answer.

Roque looked puzzled by the memory. "Well, from the way they acted, you'd have thought I'd just burned their crops and spit in their sweet tea. They wouldn't give me the time of day, much less a job. And ever since, just about everybody in town has had it in for me. I don't understand it. I always thought small towns were supposed to be so friendly, but this one sure isn't, at least to me. It's like I've got a black cloud over my head following me most wherever I go, or a *Kick Me* sign taped to my back."

"That's too bad," Susana said. It really was too bad, but also perfectly understandable.

"So how did you end up living on Mr. Mendoza's lot?" she asked.

"Well, at this point Cisco was still on the ranch with Dirk, because I didn't have any place to take him. I was eating breakfast one morning at that Czech bakery in town—you know, the one that sells kolaches and breakfast tacos?"

She chuckled. "Yeah, I know it. That's my family's place."

His face brightened. "No kidding! I

love that place. Nobody ever sneers at me there. Everyone's so friendly. So anyway, I was there one morning, eating my chorizo kolaches, when Mr. Mendoza came in to get breakfast tacos for his crew. We got to talking, and when he found out I didn't have a place to stay and needed a pasture for my horse, he offered to rent me his lot. He hooked me up with a job, too. It's construction, not cowboying, but it's a paycheck."

That sounded like Mr. Mendoza. He'd made fun of Roque as much as anyone in town—in fact, he was the one who'd come up with the name Bobby Six-Guns—but he had a generous heart.

"I wish I could afford something better, with a real pasture for Cisco," Roque went on. "He's been my truest friend through all this, and he was Granddad's horse. On my days off, I load him up and take him out to the state park to ride him, but it's not really enough, and I feel like I'm letting him down. This morning when I went out to feed him and he wasn't there, it was like the final line in a country song. My woman done left, I got shot, I got no money and no prospects, and in the end even my horse ran away."

He said it with a smile, but the smile didn't reach his eyes. However off-putting his manner might be, this was a warm-hearted, well-meaning guy. He was probably used to being popular.

"Dirk told me if I ever wanted to sell back Cisco and his gear, he'd give me a fair price," he said. "Maybe I should take him up on it. Cut my losses and leave town."

"You can't give up," said Susana. "Not after everything you've been through. You've got to stick it out."

He let out an impatient sigh. "But how? I don't get what I'm doing wrong. You heard those guys in the feed store that day. Why does everyone hate me? What about small-town friendliness and Southern hospitality and all that?"

Susana took a slow sip of coffee. "Do you really want to know?"

"Yeah, I really want to know. Give it to me straight. I can take it."

She set her mug on the table. "Okay. First of all, Southern hospitality is…complicated. Southerners are generally hospitable, yes, but they can be very insular. They protect their own against outsiders. And they don't like northern accents, especially northeastern. They hear it and their defenses go up. I know that isn't fair, but it's just the way it is. I don't think it's even a conscious reaction half the time."

He frowned. "You're saying I need to learn to talk like youse around here?"

"No! Do *not* try to do that. You'll look like a poser, or like you're making fun. That's the worst thing you can be, is an outsider making fun of the South."

"But I'm not an outsider. It's not like I don't have any connection to this place. I had Granddad."

"He was a lifelong rancher, from a long line of lifelong ranchers, well-known and respected in the community. You're not his blood. You're just a kid who used to visit over the summer."

"But I *left* the North. I *chose* to be here. Doesn't that count for something? I want to live here, get my own place. I said so right from the start, when I was looking for work."

"Yeah, I'm afraid that wouldn't score you any points either. A lot of rich outsiders are moving to rural areas, buying up the land and driving up the price of real estate. The locals don't like it. They figured you're one of those people."

He made a scoffing sound. "I'm not rich."

"I know, but you look like you are. Which brings me to your clothes."

He looked down at himself. "What's wrong with my clothes?"

She ran her eyes down his long lean frame. He'd taken off his coat and draped it over the back of his chair, and set his cowboy hat carefully on the table, upside down. He knew proper cowboy hat etiquette, anyway. Henry Hager must have taught him that.

"Let's start with your coat," she began.

He laid a protective hand on it as if she'd just said, *Let's douse your coat with kerosene and set fire to it*. "Hey," he said. "I'll have you know this is a very practical coat. It's oilskin, which means the rain just runs right off it, and it's got a saddle gusset so you can wear it on horseback."

"It's a beautiful coat," Susana admitted. "I wouldn't mind having one myself. But it's too new, and it looks like it came off the set of *The Man from Snowy River*."

He frowned. "Is that a cowboy movie? Should I watch it?"

"If you want, but only because it's a good movie. But it's about cowboys in Australia, so do *not* try to imitate the accent."

"Okay, got it. What else?"

"I would lose the turkey feather in the hat. Too extra."

He gave her a pleading look, followed by an exaggerated sigh, and plucked the feather out of the band. "Done. What else? What about my shirt? Anything wrong with it?"

He spread his arms out, inviting her to take a good look, which she did. Hmm. Broad shoulders and chest, tapering to a lean waist…

She forced her attention to the shirt, a flannel button-down in a rich autumnal plaid—red, black, caramel and cream.

"The shirt's fine," she said. "Plaid button-downs are always good, and solid button-downs. Stay away from snap shirts. They're not worn in this part of the state, and they'd make you look like you just came from the rodeo. T-shirts are fine, as long as they don't have offensive slogans. Stick with solids. Stay away from logos. Too controversial. Even tractor preferences stir up strong feelings. We don't want you getting sucked into a hot debate about John Deere versus Kubota versus Farmall."

"No snaps, no slogans, no tractors. What else? What about my jeans? Are they okay?"

He stuck his feet out, his booted heels landing with solid thumps on Susana's kitchen floor. It was another opportunity for a lingering gaze, this time at long well-muscled, denim-clad thighs.

"Your jeans are fine, too," Susana said briskly. "But your boots are another story."

He gave her a wounded look. "Oh, come on. You're not going to hate on the boots, too, are you? I paid a lot of money for these boots."

"Too much money. Those are dancing boots. They're too pretty and pricey for mucking around on a ranch. You need some plain calfskin Ropers for everyday wear."

"All right," he said grudgingly. "What else?"

"Get yourself a rain gauge and put it up. Next time it rains, see how much is in it. Then when you go to the feed store, be ready to tell everyone how much rain you got at your place, and ask how much they got at theirs. Texans care about rain."

"Okaaaayy," he said. "Anything else?"

She thought awhile before answering. This next part wouldn't be easy to explain.

"All those things are externals," she said at last. "They're important, but they're not the main thing. The truth is, Texas is a state of mind. There's more to being a cowboy, or a Texan, than putting on your spurs and chaps and swaggering around. To become a fully naturalized Texan, you have to pay your dues. When you're at the feed store, don't talk, listen. Those old guys standing around the cash register know a thing or two. Listen in, and smile and nod once in a while. Don't try to contribute right away. Let them get used to you. Self-assurance is good, but don't be cocky."

"Smile, nod, keep my mouth shut. Got it."

"I'm serious, Roque. This is a big deal. You remember that movie I was talking about? *The Man from Snowy River*? There's this scene where these old ranchers come to the hero's house after his father dies and tell him he has to leave his high country ranch and go work in the lowlands as a hired man, and earn the right to be up in the mountains, like his father did before him. Only it sounds way cooler in the movie because the guy says it in a Scottish accent."

"Scottish? I thought you said they were Australian."

"Yeah, I guess settlers were still coming to Australia from different places back then and the accent hadn't jelled yet. But the point is, the old ranchers were right. The stuff you have to learn can't be put on a checklist and ticked off. It's intangible. It has to be experienced. You have to be patient and humble and willing to learn. If you do, then maybe a rancher around here will take notice of you and give you a job. And if you work hard, you'll learn new skills and get a good reputation in the community, and maybe Dirk will change his mind about you."

He thought awhile. "Okay," he said at last. "I'm not sure I get what you're saying, but I guess that's the point. You're the one who lives here and works here and knows how things are, and I'm going to take your word for it."

"Good," said Susana. "I hope it helps."

But she knew it wasn't enough.

She could imagine Roque as that hyperactive kid who wanted to be a cowboy, who couldn't settle down to anything until he came to his granddad's ranch. She wondered how things might have turned out if his father had bitten the bullet and paid to keep flying him to Texas for the summers. Maybe he would have stayed on at the ranch once he grew up and never gone through those wild years. And with his help, maybe the Hager Ranch wouldn't have struggled so much financially.

Roque downed the last of his coffee, set the mug down and got to his feet. "Well, thanks for the coffee and sympathy, and the advice. I guess I better get on home."

Susana stood, too. She could hear the forced cheerfulness in his tone. She didn't like sending him back to his lonely, cheerless quarters in an old horse trailer. She felt as if she were tossing a stray dog back out into the cold.

She walked him outside. The temperature was definitely rising. Looked like the Extreme Winter Weather Event was finally coming to an end.

"Oh, hey, I'm going to have to leave Cisco here for the time being," Roque said. "At least until the roads clear some more. I didn't want to hitch up my trailer and try to deal with all that in this ice and snow."

"Please don't worry about it," said Susana. "You can keep Cisco here as long as you like."

Those were rash words, but somehow she knew Roque wouldn't abuse her trust.

"Thanks. I'll reimburse you for his feed."

He rubbed his chin. "Look, I don't know how you'd feel about this, but if you'd rather not wait for that plumber, I could check out those busted pipes myself."

"Oh! Well, um, do you have any plumbing experience?"

He grinned. "I'm a man of many skills. I've worked as a commercial fisherman, offshore roughneck, frame carpenter and backyard mechanic. I've done demolition work and welding, too. And I'm a certified journeyman plumber in the state of New Jersey."

"Well—"

"I won't charge you anything," he said. "It's the least I can do after everything you've done for me, and it's not like I've got anything better to do. Work's canceled until the roads are clear."

"Well—"

"Call my boss if you want," he went on. "Zachary Diaz. He's a building contractor. I don't do plumbing on the job in Texas, because I'm not certified here, but he could vouch for me that I know what I'm doing."

"You work for Zac Diaz?"

"Yeah, you know him?"

Susana laughed. "He's the cousin who built my house."

"Seriously? Call him up, then, and see what he says. I'll go get my tools from the truck and crawl under the house to see what's up. If nothing else, I can give you an idea of what you'll be dealing with, repair-wise."

He was already halfway to his truck before he'd finished talking.

CHAPTER SIX

THE CRAWL SPACE under Susana's house was pretty shallow for a man of Roque's size, or of any size, but it wasn't the tightest space he'd worked in, and he'd never been claustrophobic. He scanned the layout with his flashlight and took some measurements. It looked simple enough. The pipes ran straight down the middle of the building, with the wet walls all together, and the water heater and washing machine situated in the garage across from the bathroom. With the temperature rising, water was already beginning to drip through the cracks.

He wriggled his way out, brushed the worst of the mud and debris off himself and walked to the front porch just as Susana was coming through her front door. Small as she was, there was nothing childlike about her figure at this distance. Even through all those layers, he could see the womanly curves. He wondered how high the top of her head would reach on him. What would it be like to kiss her? Would he have to pick her up? Her waist looked small enough for him to span with his hands.

He was so busy with the imaginary kiss that he forgot to watch where he was going. He tripped on the top step and went sprawling across the porch.

"You all right?" Susana asked.

"Fine," Roque said, getting quickly to his feet.

"Well?" she asked. "What's the damage?"

"About what I expected," he said. "All the lines have visible cracks at the water supply end, but you can be sure there are hairline cracks farther down. The big cracks are the only ones dripping now, but that's just because the water can't make it the rest of the way down. Your best bet is to rip it all out and start fresh. I know that sounds drastic, but it'll be faster and cheaper in the long run."

She thought a moment, then said, "Okay. Come with me to the garage and we'll see how much PVC I have. There's a lot left over from when the house was built."

He followed her around to the garage. "Does this mean you got the go-ahead from your cousin? You'll let me do the work?"

She gave him a quick smile over her shoulder. "You're awfully eager to be given the green light on a plumbing job that you're offering to do for free."

"I don't mind. I like fixing things. And you've been so good to me and Cisco, it's the least I can do."

"In that case, go right ahead. Zac gave you a glowing recommendation."

"Glowing? Wow." Roque hadn't expected that. His boss was a taciturn guy and didn't often enthuse.

The garage had all the pipes and fittings Roque needed, plus primer and cement. No need to go to town. He could start right away.

"The well pump is in that little building in the front yard," Susana said. "It has a shutoff valve inside. I'll leave you to it and go get some work done. If you need me, it shouldn't be hard to find me."

It looked like the storm had done damage to the pump house, ripping off some of the siding and metal roofing. Roque shut off the water to the house, then took his PVC cutter and a small work light out of the tool chest in his truck and went to it.

The hardest part of the job was getting himself back underneath the house with everything he needed. Once he was situated with all his tools and supplies, the rest was pretty straightforward—time-consuming, but straightforward. As he cut away the old pipes, he tossed them out of his way toward the front of the house where he could collect them later. Then he fitted the new ones. Cold seeped up from the ground into his back and limbs, but he didn't mind. It felt good to be doing something active and constructive after so many days housebound. His phone didn't have enough juice to play any tunes, but he basically had his favorite country music playlist internalized, so he sang it to himself.

Early in the process, while he was cutting pipe away, a fluffy orange cat joined him under the house. It settled its warm weight on his chest right away, purring like a little motor. Whenever Roque shifted it off so he could ooch over to a new spot, it waited until he settled down and then got right back on again.

At last, Roque completed the final fitting and wormed his way out on his back. By now he'd been under the house for hours and felt sore and stiff. He got to his feet, arched his back and started rotating his left arm in big slow circles, trying to ease out the soreness in his shoulder and chest. He didn't bounce back as quickly as he used to before he got hurt.

It seemed bright out here after the darkness beneath the house, but the sun had started going down. A steady drip fell from the icicles along the eaves, and the snow was growing slushy underfoot.

Roque pulled out his phone, set the timer for one hour and returned it to his back pocket. Then he took a good look around. All along the horizon, the leafless trees made a smudge of black against the sky. The snow was retreating from the ground, leaving bare brown patches in the pens. Over in the arena, Susana was working with a horse. He stood a moment watching her. After four days of not laying eyes on another human being, it felt good having someone else around, even at a distance.

A meow drew his gaze down. The orange cat had followed him out from under the house. It looked him in the eye, waggled its rear and launched its body up.

Roque was glad he'd had at least a moment's warning. The cat landed on his shoulder and wrapped itself around his neck like a fur collar. It rubbed its face against the side of Roque's head, purring. Roque stroked its ears and throat.

"Cat," he said, "that is one fine woman over there."

She had a calm energy about her that he imagined animals would respond well to. She was a restful person, open and kind, decent and sweet. He thought suddenly of Layla. There'd been a core of selfishness to his ex-girlfriend. What Layla wanted, she took, whether it was the last slice of pizza that Roque had already packed for his lunch the next day, or an investment banker named Broderick. She took without a second thought or a moment's regret for the cost to anyone else. Roque could see that now. But she'd sure charmed him in the beginning.

He turned his back on Susana and headed back to the garage, the orange cat riding on his shoulders. He'd seen some extra siding and roofing in there that matched the well house. Might as well repair the damage while waiting for the PVC cement to cure.

But his mind kept straying back to that small graceful form and thick swinging braid.

He shook his head, trying to get rid of the image. He couldn't afford to go down that road. That feeling when Layla had left, like an excavator had carved a chunk out of his chest and left him bleeding, the pain of it mingling with the pain of the bullet wounds—he couldn't go through that again.

It wasn't just timing that linked the breakup to his injury. If Layla hadn't left him, he wouldn't have been buying a fifth of Scotch at 3:00 a.m. to begin with. She hadn't pulled the trigger, but whenever he dreamed about the shooting, it was her face he saw behind the 9-millimeter.

Anyway, he didn't suppose Susana would stay single for long. Someday soon, one of those uncle's neighbor's nephews was going to take a good look at her and decide he could live with the twice-a-day horse feedings.

Meanwhile, he'd be busy making a success of this cowboy thing. A cowboy was solitary by nature—a man and his horse, underneath a sky so immense that he couldn't get lonely. Or if he did, he had only to remind himself that loneliness was better than a hole in your heart. The feeling would pass. He just had to wait it out.

SUSANA HAD LET a lot of horse-grooming tasks slide during the snowstorm, and now she was playing catch-up. Damascus, a sorrel gelding, had managed to get several big cockleburs caught in his mane and tail, and his forelock was a solid mass of cockleburs held together by hair. She used some straight-jaw pliers to crush the burs into small pieces, then worked them out. Damascus had unusually fine forelock hair, and when she finished, it was all fluffed up into a ball of golden fuzz between his ears. His roommate, Amadeus, didn't have many burs, but he did have plenty of jumping cactus caught on his haunches and face. Jumping cactus didn't really jump, but it sure seemed to. Pieces of it could break off at the slightest touch and stick to anyone or anything that passed by. Like cockleburs, it was a real pain to have in a horse pen. Susana had cleared out all the prickly stuff when she'd first run her fencing, but it had crept in again from the uncleared area at the back. She needed to get out there with the tractor and shredder. Well, what she *really* needed was to clear a wide swath behind the pastures, and get the uncleared area in shape for trail rides. But for the immediate future, clearing the burs and cactus from the pastures themselves was ambitious enough.

Pirko kept her company, trotting briskly at her side.

Susana deburred and decactused all the horses from that area. Then she brought out Royal, a feisty little Morgan, and put him on the walker for some exercise. Roque's bay, Cisco, was still in the arena. She moved him to a spare pasture that she used for isolating sick or hurt horses and gave him some hay.

She felt a little funny, leaving Roque to his own devices all this time, but he could find her easily enough if he needed to, and he knew what he was doing. Her cousin Zac's endorsement hadn't actually been glowing, but it had been good enough for her.

"He's not bad," Zac had said when Susana had called and explained the situation. "He doesn't show up to work hungover, and he does know what he's doing when it comes to plumbing. Framing and drywall, too. He's a decent worker. The only complaint I have about him is that he sings country music at the top of his lungs in that Yankee accent of his. Other than that, he's an okay guy."

She did her best to concentrate on her own work and not dwell on the fact that her girlhood crush was on her property doing home repairs at this very moment.

And there was certainly plenty of her own work to be done—feet to be picked, tack to be cleaned and polished, horse blankets to be put away. Meriadoc's blanket was filthy. She didn't have time now to clean it thoroughly, so she draped it over a metal sawhorse, brushed off the excess dirt, hosed it down with water from the windmill and left it to dry. By now the sky had cleared enough to let some thin wintry sunlight through.

Then she took Leda, a Thoroughbred mare, to the arena for some longeing. Afterward, as she walked Leda back to her pen, she saw Roque doing something or other near the well house. She hoped that meant he was finished.

She shut Leda's gate. "Come on, Pirko," she said. "Let's check in and get an update."

As she drew near, she heard singing. Loud singing. She recognized the familiar blues strain of "Folsom Prison Blues," but Johnny Cash never sounded like *that*. Roque's pitch was right on target, and the timbre of his voice was good, but that accent! Did he lack self-awareness, or simply not care? He got points for enthusiasm, anyway. He never messed up the lyrics, and he even did guitar sounds in between the verses.

He broke off abruptly when he saw her. "Oh, hey there," he said cheerfully, with no trace of embarrassment.

"Hey," she said. "Did you replace the siding on the well house? Thanks. You didn't have to do that."

"It was no trouble. The materials were right there in the garage, and I had to wait for the PVC cement to cure anyway."

Just then, an alarm went off on his phone. "Speaking of which," he said as he took it out of his back pocket and turned off the sound. Then he grinned at her. "All right, this is it. You ready for the moment of truth?"

"Sure. What do you want me to do?"

"Go inside and open up the taps. Check under the sinks. Water heater and washer hookup, too. If any of the interior pipes are busted, or if you hear gushing behind the walls, come to the door and yell out, and I'll shut it off again. I'll check under the house."

She went to the kitchen and turned both handles. It took only a minute or so for the water to reach the tap. Some gurgling, a trickle, a few bursts of air—and then a steady stream of water. No leaks under the sink, or in the bathroom, or at the water heater or washing machine. Pirko followed her around the house, hurrying alongside, peering under the sinks with her and wagging excitedly as if she understood exactly what was going on.

Back outside, she found Roque crouching by the crawl space, peering under the house. He straightened and asked, "So what's the verdict?"

"All good inside," she said.

He leaped over the steps onto the porch. "All good under here, too. Yeah!"

He held out his fist. She gave the knuckles a light bump.

"Thank you so much for doing this, Roque. This is such a load off my mind. I'm going to be able to wash dishes tonight! And clean the kitchen, and do laundry…"

Roque chuckled. "Boy, you sure know how to celebrate."

"Well, after all that, I'm going to have a nice hot bath."

"Good for you! Man, I miss baths. I've just got a little shower stall at my place.

It gets the job done, but it isn't the same. I shouldn't complain, though. I never lost water, and I had enough propane for hot showers, and for washing dishes if I'd wanted to do that."

"You didn't? Wash dishes?"

"There was nothing to wash. I didn't have anything to eat the past four days but those noodles in Styrofoam cups."

"Well then, can I offer you a meal? I have a fridge full of leftovers—sausage, ham, baked chicken, mashed potatoes, gravy, green beans, sweet potato casserole, kolaches, pecan pie…"

As if on cue, Roque's stomach let out a loud growl. He clapped a hand to it and gave her a soulful look. "That sounds fantastic. But I don't want to impose."

"Impose? You're the reason I have running water. Besides, I need help clearing out all the food. My mom brought it for me for Christmas, and it's way too much for one person. I kept the fridge door mostly shut through the outages, so it's still good, but it won't be for much longer. You'd be doing me a favor if you stayed and helped me work through it all."

"Well, if you're sure. Yeah, I'll stay. Thanks."

Susana looked at the sky, then at her watch. "I have to feed horses first, though. I need to get it done before the sun sets."

"No problem," said Roque. "It'll go quicker with two of us, right? I'll help you out."

He reached for his coat, which was draped over the porch rail.

"Oh, no!" Susana said. "Your beautiful coat. It's all mucked up."

Roque shrugged. "Yeah, that's what happens when you scooch around under the house on your back. You said it looked too new, right? Now it's broken in."

She led him to the feed barn and opened the doors. "Start filling those blue buckets with feed from this first bin, two scoops per bucket, and set them in the truck bed. Yellow buckets get high-fat feed, and red and green get other additives. I'll take care of those."

"You got it, boss."

Pirko kept them company. When Roque's bin ran out of feed, he picked up a fifty-pound bag, expertly opened the string-sealed end and emptied the feed into the bin as if it were no heavier than a box of cereal.

Susana watched in silent admiration and envy. Whenever she had to empty those bags into the bins, it was a different matter. At her height, it was all she could do to hoist one up to the top of the bin and keep it in place while the feed poured out. That didn't stop her from doing it, but it sure made for a nice change, having a large, strong, energetic man on the place to handle the heavy work.

"Looks like you're going to have to make another run to the feed store soon," Roque said as he flattened the empty feed sack and stacked it with the others.

"Yeah. I stocked up as much as I could before the storm, but I don't have the storage space for more than a few days' worth. That means I have to go to the feed store twice a week."

"You really need that bigger barn."

"I know it. I've thought about putting up a big metal shell of a building and finishing the inside as I'm able, but that wouldn't exactly be cheap, and it isn't what I want."

"What do you want?"

"A raised center aisle barn with twelve stalls, plus a feed room, a tack room and a wash station. That way I could stall some horses, and charge more money than I do for pasture-only horses. Of course, then I'd have to turn out the stall horses and exercise them, but with the extra income, maybe I could finally afford to hire some help."

She loaded the last of the buckets into the truck bed and opened the driver's door. Roque stood on the other side of the truck, passenger door open, staring at the bench seat pulled up as far as it would go, with the cushion on the driver's seat that gave Susana a couple of inches of extra height, and another one for her back to push her forward.

"How about if I drive?" he asked.

Susana chuckled. "Yeah, I guess that would be best."

They switched places. Roque let the seat all the way back before climbing in.

Pirko was delighted to have Roque along in the truck, even though it meant she had to ride in the middle this time. She licked Roque, then licked Susana, and finally took her place, staring straight ahead like she always did.

Roque started the truck.

"You haven't said it yet," said Susana.

"Said what?"

"That I'm short."

Roque shrugged. "I figured you already knew."

The feeding did go faster with two people. Roque was a good, quick, cheerful worker, and he clearly knew his way around horses. Henry Hager had taught him well.

At one pen, he pointed at the horse, a dun roan called Montford, and asked, "Does this guy look a little lame to you?"

"Yeah, he does," said Susana. "Let's go check him out."

She grabbed her hoof pick out of the glove compartment, then slid between the bars of the gate and got Montford to lift his front left leg. "Yep, there's a stone in here, all right," she said.

She dug out the stone and set Montford's leg gently back on the ground.

"Good eye," she told Roque.

"Thanks," he said. "We make a pretty good team, don't we?"

"Yeah," said Susana. "We do, actually."

AT EACH STOP, Susana told Roque about the horses, their personalities and their histories.

"This is Lester. He was skin and bones when I first brought him home from auction, but he's filled out nicely. His roommate over there is Napoleon. See Napoleon's fetlocks, and how big he is, and the shape of his face? I'm pretty sure he's part draft. He's a great riding horse—nothing ever spooks him… That black-and-white paint is called Oreo, and the piebald with him is his brother, Peanut. They belong to a married couple who pick them up on weekends and take them riding… This chestnut fellow is called Barrymore. His owner never comes to see him. Always pays his rent on time, but I feel sorry for him—the horse, I mean. He's so well trained, too. It's a shame… The palomino is Daisy. She was a rescue. The place she came from must have had a stallion nearby and not very good fencing, because she was in foal when I got her, though I didn't know it at the time. The vet thinks she's due in a few months... And this little Arabian is Meriadoc. He's the first horse I ever rode, and the first one I bought once I had my own place. He belonged to my grandparents' neighbors. After the neighbors died, their kids sold the land. Nobody wanted Meriadoc, so I took him. He's been around as long as I can remember, so he's got to be at least twenty-five. He's prone to colic, and he has trouble keeping weight on. He needs special feed and hoof supplement, and he takes as much care as my highest-paying clients' horses without bringing in any income at all, but he can't help that, can you, boy?"

The little Arabian lifted his nose from his feeder and nuzzled Susana in the shoulder. Roque felt something catch in his chest. She was so generous and openhearted.

By the time they'd finished, the sun had gone down, and a wintry twilight had settled. Roque drove the truck back to the feed barn, and they unloaded the buckets.

"I feel like I got away with something because we finished so quickly," Susana said as they walked back to the house.

"And I feel like I used to after a day on the ranch with Granddad," said Roque. "Starving. I'm looking forward to that dinner."

It was such a luxury for Susana to stand at the kitchen sink and wash her hands in plenty of warm soapy water. The power was still on, so she got busy heating food while Roque took his turn cleaning up.

When they finally sat down to eat, the small table was crammed to full capacity with turkey, dressing, sausage, ham, two noodle dishes, a broccoli and rice casserole, more rice with cinnamon on top, a sweet potato casserole, pickled beets, homemade rolls and more.

Roque sat there a moment, taking it all in. "Man! This is a feast, all right. I can't remember the last time I saw this much food at one time."

"Eat as much as you want, but save room for dessert. We've got kolaches, cream cheese rolls, a chocolate sheet cake and a strudel. On second thought, don't worry about saving room. If you're too full for dessert, you can just take some home with you, and any other leftovers you're interested in."

He picked up his plate and started helping himself. "I'll take anything you want to send with me. Look at all this *meat*!"

"Yes, Christmas dinner is a three-meat meal in Czech households. When I was growing up, it was one-meat meals for every day, two-meat meals for Sunday lunch and three-meat meals for holidays. My parents and grandparents still follow that rule."

"I like that rule." He pointed to a bowl filled with little bundles wrapped in cornhusks. "And tamales? Are they a part of traditional Czech cuisine?"

"They are in this part of the country. The story goes that decades back, a home extension agent showed Czech housewives how to make them and a tradition was born! This batch was made by my stepcousin Linda, Zac's mother."

Roque unwrapped a tamale. "So you've got step-cousins, too, huh?"

"Yes. My great-great-grandfather on the

Labaj side was widowed with five kids, and he married a widow with three kids of her own. That's where the Diaz connection comes from. And the Diazes are related to the Mendozas, but the Mendozas aren't directly related to me."

Roque chuckled. "That sounds like my family. I'm Sicilian and Corsican on my mom's side, and my dad's people were Portuguese. They were all small farmers and herdsmen for the most part, and once they came to the States, they went right on gardening in the city. Raised their own vegetables and herbs in pots on their apartment balconies."

"Oh, I love that. It's special to belong to a community with a strong ethnic identity, isn't it? You ought to see Novak, the farming and ranching town my parents come from. It's like a little Czech colony in Texas. It's all Vrbas and Labajes and Vlahoses out there. They live on land that's been in their families since their ancestors first came over. There's a little church, too. A small Protestant denomination called Czech Moravian Brethren."

Roque chuckled again. "I know about

small Protestant denominations. I'm Lusitanian Catholic Apostolic Evangelical myself. Do you see your extended family much?"

"Not as often as I'd like. Novak's an hour away, and there's always so much work to be done here that it's hard to get away that far."

They worked their way through the food and lingered at the table afterward, talking and talking. At last, Roque pushed back his chair and let out a sigh.

"That," he said, "was an excellent meal. Thank you."

"I'm glad you liked it. How about dessert?"

"I'm game. But maybe we could do night check on the horses first. Let the food settle a bit."

They walked rather than driving this time, Pirko scampering ahead of them and then circling back. Everything was as it should be. The few early stars were sharp and clear in the deep blue sky.

When they went back to the house, Susana said, "I have a proposal to make."

Her upturned face looked earnest and hopeful in the moonlight.

"What is it?" Roque asked.

"A trade. Twenty hours of work a week in exchange for Cisco's board. I have more work here than I can handle by myself, and you have too much time on your hands. You can handle fencing and rougher work for me, freeing me up to work more with the horses and get ahead. In exchange, I can give you not just board for your horse, but advice and credibility. There are a lot of farmers and ranchers in this town whose goodwill you're going to need if you ever want to make a life here. I can show you how to do that, and provide the experience you need, and help with the intangibles. Cisco will have a roomy pasture and you'll have a local place to ride him—especially once we get those trails constructed. So what do you think?"

Roque grinned and stuck out his hand. "I think you got yourself a deal."

CHAPTER SEVEN

SUSANA SPENT THE earliest part of the next morning wondering if Roque would show up for work, or if he'd beg off, or even stand her up without calling, leaving her to track him down and wrest an explanation out of him, like a client skipping out on his board payment and then dodging her calls. The arrangement they'd made seemed too good to be true. *He* seemed too good to be true. She kept an eye on the clock, and prepared herself to be disappointed. It had happened often enough in the past.

But he came, right on time.

Her heart gave a strange throb when she looked out the kitchen window and saw his truck pulling into the driveway. Pirko must have heard the engine, because her ears pricked and she trotted to the front door.

Susana put on her coat and stepped out onto the porch, Pirko at her side. Roque parked his truck and came her way with that long stride of his, holding a big commuter mug in one hand and a sturdy-looking portable speaker in the other, and wearing his oilskin drover coat with most of yesterday's mud brushed off.

He grinned as he held up the speaker. "So's I can listen to my tunes," he said. "Hope that's okay."

"I don't mind if the horses don't mind," she said. "Come inside the house for a minute. There's something I want to take care of before we get started."

She led him to her office—a tiny second bedroom—and handed him a clipboard with a sheet of paper on it.

"What's this supposed to be?" he asked.

"A contract," she said. "For our agreement."

"A contract! What do we need a contract for? We hashed everything out last night. I work for you twenty hours a week in exchange for boarding my horse. Simple."

"Simple or not, it still has to be formalized. If there's one thing I've learned from all the small business owners in my family, it's always make a contract. Get the exact terms down on paper with no ambiguity. Verbal agreements have a way of going south unless they're put in writing. People forget, or change their minds, or realize they had different interpretations of things all along. This way, everyone's protected."

"All right, if you say so. You got a pen?"

"Roque! Were you even listening? You can't sign it before you read it."

"Why not? You put something sketchy in there? Does the party of the second part have to hand over his firstborn child or something?"

She folded her arms over her chest. "Well, there's one way to find out, isn't there? Go on. Read it."

Roque let out an exaggerated sigh, took a seat on Susana's desk chair and started to read.

She kept a close watch on his face and knew the moment he'd reached that one paragraph, the one she'd agonized over for nearly an hour. He stopped, frowned, reread, and finally looked up at her with those dark eyes that had haunted her memory for an embarrassing number of years.

"Keep our relationship on a professional footing?" he quoted.

He didn't seem offended or disappointed or—what would have been worst of all—mocking. Just quizzical. She'd worked hard to strike the proper tone, one that didn't sound as if she expected him to come on to her, or believed he was already attracted to her—much less that she was already attracted to him, and needed something concrete to rein herself in so she wouldn't let her heart run away with her and make a fool of her. That ridiculous girlhood crush hadn't exactly dissolved once she'd seen him in the flesh all these years later.

"It's pretty standard stuff," she said, keeping her voice neutral.

He looked back at the text. "All right, if you say so. I see you made it a month-to-month deal."

"Yes, I thought that was best not to lock ourselves into a long-term agreement. This way, either of us can end the arrangement at any time by giving thirty days' notice."

"That makes sense," said Roque. "Now where's that pen?"

"Are you sure you're ready to sign? If

there's anything there you don't agree with, we can talk it over. This is the time to make alterations, not five months down the road."

"Nope, looks good to me. Hand me a pen so's I can put my John Hancock on here and get to work. As Granddad used to say, we're burning daylight."

She gave him a pen. He signed with a flourish and handed it back to her.

"There," he said. "You want I should get it notarized?"

"That isn't necessary," she said, taking the sheet out of the clipboard and laying it on the desk. "I'll have copies made, one for your records and one to post in the feed barn. I'll keep the original in my files."

"Great. *Now* can I get to work?"

"Hold on." She handed the clipboard back to him. "You still need to log your hours."

"Log my hours? I don't need to log my hours. I may not be a math prodigy, but I can keep track of twenty hours a week."

"This is *how* we keep track, with a time log. I have to record all my financial transactions for tax purposes, including barter arrangements." She pointed. "See? It's set up like a calendar. Here's today's block. Just write down the time you show up and the time you leave."

"Hmm, I don't know. Sounds kind of complicated to me. You sure you can trust me to get it right? Maybe you ought to install a biometric attendance system. Scan my retina, take a DNA sample."

She smiled, then said sternly, "Log the time."

He gave another exaggerated sigh, scribbled the time in the correct block and handed the clipboard to her.

"There," he said. "Now can the aforesaid party of the second part get to work?"

"You'd better. You just logged your start time. You are officially on the clock."

He clapped his hands together. "Great! So what do you want I should do today?"

"We'll start with feeding. Last night I just had you handle the buckets for the horses that have a standard diet, but some of our clients have special dietary needs. I've got a chart posted in the feed barn that you can consult. I'll show you what it all means and where everything's kept."

They walked to the feed barn together

in the early morning stillness. Roque opened the double doors, and Susana hung the clipboard with the time sheet from a nail on the wall.

The sun was just peeking over the tips of the cedar trees when they loaded the last of the buckets into the bed of the truck. Roque drove again.

At their first stop, he took the two pens on the right while Susana took the two on the left. Pirko seemed confused. She scampered after Susana, then spun around and followed Roque, then hurried back again.

"Check it out! No ice chunks in the water today," Roque called from his side.

"I know! The winter storm is well and truly over."

It was nice having company for morning feeding. It was also nice finishing the job in half the time it usually took.

There was still some snow left on the ground in low or shady spots. By the time they drove back to the feed barn, the rising sun was casting long thin blue shadows of the fence posts and trees.

"What should I do now?" Roque asked

as he stacked the last of the empty buckets beside the feed barn.

"I'd like you to start clearing brush and weeds and cactus from the corners of some of the pens. I've got the loppers, the bow saw and a shovel ready in the wheelbarrow. Cut the mesquite limbs and dig up the cactus. Do not—I repeat do not—leave a single cactus fragment behind, or it'll regenerate and grow a whole new root system. The cockleburs should come up easily enough by hand, but make sure to get the actual burs picked up from the ground so they don't reseed. And be careful to gather all the mesquite limbs. Those thorns can be pretty nasty, and I don't want the horses stepping on them. Then load everything into the wheelbarrow and take it to the burn pile."

Roque pulled a pair of leather work gloves out of his back pocket and put them on, then followed her out to the wheelbarrow. "Ready when you are."

She led him to the pen that Damascus and Amadeus shared.

"All the pens on this side back up to that scrubby area," she said, pointing. "I cleared the brush out initially, but it's been creeping back in through the fence. The worst of it is in this first pen. Take care of it first. Amadeus is nosy, so I'll take him out and put him on the walker while you work, but I'll leave Damascus here. He won't bother you."

"Sounds good." Roque set up his speaker on a cedar corner post and pulled up his music on his phone. Susana left him to it and went to work exercising some of the horses.

Roque's playlist was…eclectic. From the arena, Susana could hear strains of classic country, rockabilly, outlaw country, bluegrass and honky-tonk. Roque sang along with every song, in full voice, with great enthusiasm. He knew every word, every note. It was really something to hear Hank Jr.'s "A Country Boy Can Survive" sung in a New Jersey accent.

Now and then she saw him taking the wheelbarrow to the burn pile and emptying it. She was working with Leda on longeing when he came to her and said, "All right, I'm all done in that first pen. You want I should start on the next one over?"

He'd taken off his coat and his overshirt

and was down to a T-shirt now. The man had an impressive set of guns.

"You're finished? Already?"

"Yeah."

"The whole pen?"

"That's right. You want to come check my work?"

"Might as well."

She switched out the longe line with a lead rope and secured Leda to the fence, then followed Roque back to the pen.

The brush and cactus and cockleburs were gone without a trace. Roque had even smoothed the soil over the spot where he'd grubbed out the cactus.

He grinned. "Told you."

She gave him a stern look. "Hey. What did I tell you about being cocky?"

"Oh, right. Sorry. What I meant to say is, thank you kindly, ma'am."

"What did I tell you about trying to sound Southern?"

"Sheesh! Okay, okay. What I *really* meant to say is, thanks. Hey, check out Damascus! He's standing in the exact spot where all the cockleburs used to be."

Susana chuckled. "Probably disappointed that he can't get them stuck in his forelock and watch me take them out anymore."

Roque stood with his hands in his back pockets, surveying his work. Her glance wandered back to his arms, with their well-defined masses and ridges of muscle. His left forearm had some thick scarring, raised and red, with irregular edges.

He caught her looking. "From the accident," he said.

She felt her cheeks growing warm. "Sorry," she said. "Didn't mean to stare."

"It's all right. I'm not self-conscious about it."

He straightened the arm and tugged the sleeve of his T-shirt up over a shapely deltoid marked by a reddish, roundish scar with puckered edges. "This was the first bullet," he said. "And this—" he pulled the neck of his shirt down and to the left "— is the second. Plowed right into the pectoral muscle and then glanced off a rib and missed my heart. Doc said I was lucky."

Susana didn't know what to say. Roque was so big and strong, so laughing and carefree, as if nothing could hurt him.

But some stranger had put two bullets in him and almost ended his life. An inch or two over on that chest wound, and Roque would have gone straight out of this world without ever coming back to Texas. She never would have seen him again, never would have known what had become of the boy at the Persimmon Festival with his funny accent and heart-melting smile.

He let go of his shirt collar.

"So you want me to move on to the next pen?" he asked. "That looks like a monster mesquite stump in the back corner."

"It is. I'd planned on burning it out, but the drought put a stop to that. Now the tree's starting to come back."

"I saw a chainsaw in your garage. I could dig around the stump and use the chainsaw to cut up the roots and then pull it out with the tractor."

"That chainsaw isn't running. Just concentrate on the smaller brush for now, and take off those suckers from the mesquite stump so it doesn't get out of control."

"You're the boss," Roque said.

They both went back to work. Susana

was doctoring a horse's hooves for thrush when Roque came back.

"I found the problem with your chainsaw," he said. "The carburetor's all clogged up. I can rebuild it, but I'll need to get the right rebuild kit, or maybe you'd rather I got a new carburetor. The chain looks pretty dull, too. I can sharpen it for you if you've got a file, but it's a good idea to have a spare chain on hand. You want I should go to the hardware store and take care of it?"

He looked eager and pleased with himself, but she felt a twinge of irritation.

"I said not to worry about the chainsaw, remember?" she said. "I told you to get that second pen cleared."

"Oh, I finished that about fifteen minutes ago. You want to see?"

For the second time that day, she followed him to the pen to check his work. Sure enough, the brush and cactus were all cleared, and there wasn't a single cactus frond or stray stick left on the ground. Nothing left but that big mesquite stump, now stripped of its suckers, ugly and sprawling with its spreading roots and the remains of multiple trunks.

He was grinning at her, like a child waiting to be praised.

"Nice job," she said. "So you really think you can fix the chainsaw?"

"I know I can. I worked as a logger in Oregon for a while and I know about chainsaw maintenance. I can go to town and get the parts right now. And once it's running, I don't see why we can't start tackling that jungle behind the back fence, and put in those trails, and start charging people for trail rides, and making the money you need for your big barn."

"Hold on there, cowboy. I can think of plenty of reasons why we can't immediately start doing all that. For one thing, there are three more pens that still need the brush cleared out of them."

"The chainsaw would make quick work of the mesquite limbs," Roque put in.

"Most of the mesquite limbs are less than two inches across. And the chainsaw wouldn't help much with the cockleburs and cactus. For another thing, you've already worked a lot of hours today, and constructing the trails is going to be a big job. I don't want to get started on that until I know I'm ready to follow through."

Roque rubbed his chin. "How about if I go ahead and sign out for today, and take care of the chainsaw sort of unofficially, on my own time?"

"I can't let you do that, Roque. I have to keep my books in order. I told you that."

He sighed. "All right, you're the boss. How about first thing tomorrow, then? I can go to town as soon as the hardware store opens, get the parts for the chainsaw and go to work on it."

Susana thought about that, then said, "No. I have a better idea. You come back here tomorrow and get the rest of those pens cleared. Then on Friday, we'll go to town together. I have errands to run, and you need a proper pair of work boots. We'll take care of it all in one trip. It's time the people of this town found out that you work for me now."

CHAPTER EIGHT

"Our first stop is Waelder's Saddle Shop," Susana said. "I need to pick up some tack that Tom's been mending for me. He also carries a line of inexpensive calfskin Ropers, so we'll get you a pair. Then we'll head over to the feed store and stock up on feed and hay for the week. After that, we'll hit Darcy's Hardware. You can look for the parts you need for the chainsaw while I find some fence clips. And what are you going to be like in those places?"

"Humble and polite," said Roque.

"And what are you going to do?"

"Smile and nod. Listen more than I talk."

"Are you going to say anything about how you want to buy land in this area?"

"No."

"Are you going to brag about your riding and roping skills?"

"No."

"If someone asks you a yes-or-no question, how are you going to answer?"

"With yes, sir, and no, sir. Or yes, ma'am, and no, ma'am."

She nodded, apparently satisfied for now.

She was letting Roque drive her truck again. It seemed to him that she enjoyed being a passenger, because it gave her a chance to check out other people's properties as they drove past. She had one leg folded underneath her again. Once in a while, she'd drop a comment about the farms and ranches she was seeing.

"Looks like the Blanchards lost the roof of their porch," she said. "It must have collapsed under the weight of the snow... The Talbot brothers are out in their orchard, taking the frost wrap off their persimmon trees. I hope the trees are all right. The persimmon is our town fruit. There won't be much of a Persimmon Festival this year if all the persimmon trees are dead."

"Oh yeah, the Persimmon Festival! I remember that. Granddad used to take me."

"I know," Susana said.

Something in her voice made him look at her. She was turned away from him, staring out the window.

"What do you mean you know?" he asked.

"I mean I remember. My parents' shop had a booth at the festival. I used to help sell persimmon kolaches every year…and you used to buy them."

She remembered him? It had been eighteen years since he'd been to a Persimmon Festival. He must have made a big impression on her. At what point had she recognized him? Why hadn't she said anything about it earlier?

He wished she would turn around and look at him. He wanted to see her face. But she kept her back to him, with her elbow on the windowsill and that long brown braid trailing over her shoulder.

Stop it, he told himself. *You can't think of her that way. You signed a contract.*

Susana wanted to keep their relationship professional. She'd made that clear. The fact that she remembered him as a kid didn't mean anything special. She might just have a really good memory. And he was probably hard to forget, swaggering around in chaps and spurs. She was probably trying to keep from laughing at him right now.

"Yeah, I did," he said finally. "They were good."

She didn't answer. They drove in silence the rest of the way to town, and Roque parked in front of the saddle shop.

"Looks like Limestone Springs is coming to life again after the snowstorm," Susana said. "All these people are wandering around like bears waking up from hibernation."

"They sure are dressed weird," said Roque. "That guy has on a parka with flip-flops."

"Typical Texas winter wear," she said. "We do our best."

He turned off the ignition and turned to face her. "Before we get out of the truck, I should tell you that Granddad taught me to open doors for ladies, and that includes truck doors. I don't often get a chance to do it, because most women hustle on out of there before I make it over to the other side. It always makes me feel kind of uneasy, like I'm skipping a step. But if you'll sit tight, I'll come around and let you out."

She chuckled. "Henry Hager really made an impact on you, didn't he? Sure, you can open the truck door for me. But only in town, not when we're feeding horses."

So she waited in the cab while Roque came around to her side and opened the truck door. He opened the door to the saddle shop, too.

The entry bell jingled, and the scent of leather and oil washed over him as he followed her inside. A gray-haired man, with rimless spectacles perched low on his nose, was sitting in an alcove by the front window, stitching a saddle.

"Morning, Tom," Susana said.

The saddler looked at her over the top of his glasses. "Good morning, Susana. How're you? How're things at your place? Did you make it through the storm all right?"

"Pretty well. My pipes under the house all froze, though. Power stayed out so long the well pump couldn't run."

Tom nodded grimly. "That happened to

a lot of folks on well water. The plumbers are going to be raking it in, if the plumbing supplies ever get replenished. Darcy already sold out of PVC pipe and most of his fittings, and he just got his delivery this morning."

"That's too bad," said Susana. "At that rate, and with the plumbers as backed up as they are, some folks are going to be without water for a long time. I'm glad I already got mine taken care of."

"Did you, now? How'd you manage that?"

Susana nodded toward Roque. "My new hired man, here, is a journeyman plumber. He cut out all the pipe under my house and replaced it the same day."

Tom turned to Roque with a smile. "Hired man, huh? I don't think I know you, son. I'm Tom Waelder. What's your name?"

"Roque Fidalgo, sir. Nice to meet you."

As soon as the words were out of his mouth, Roque saw Tom's smile stiffen. It was like watching a wall go up. Susana was right. His accent was definitely working against him.

Tom gave him a polite nod, then walked

over to the counter and pulled out a package of tack. "Here's that bridle of yours," he said to Susana. "Good as new."

"Thank you. Just leave it by the register, please. We're not ready to check out yet. Roque needs to get some work boots."

"Okay, then. Right this way."

Tom led them down an aisle of plain men's boots. He glanced at the boots Roque had on, then did a double take.

"You didn't buy those here," he said disapprovingly.

Humble and polite, Roque reminded himself. *Humble and polite.*

"No, sir, I sure didn't," Roque said, as humbly and politely as ever he could. "I was new in town and I didn't know where to go."

"Hmm. Well, we'll get you fixed up with some plain calfskin Ropers, and you can save those fancy things for the dance hall."

While Roque tried on boots, Susana browsed around the store. He called her over when he found a pair he liked.

"What do you think?" he asked. "They plain enough for you?"

"They're perfect," she said.

"All right, then. I'll take them."

"Would you like to wear them out of the store?" asked Tom.

"Yes, sir."

Tom packed Roque's dancing boots into the box the Ropers had come in.

Susana had wandered over to some dress tack and was looking longingly at some pieces with silver conchos.

"That one with the flowers would look pretty on Daisy," Roque said.

"Yes, it would." She glanced at the price tag and sighed. "Oh well. Maybe someday."

Tom had gone back to work on the saddle. It was stamped all over the seat, stirrup leathers and saddle horn in an intricate herringbone pattern.

"Is that a custom saddle?" Roque asked.

Tom gave him another grave over-the-spectacles look. "It is," he said. "Made for a rancher in Schraeder Lake."

"Lucky man," Roque said.

He paid for the boots, and Susana paid for the mended tack.

"That was a good start," she said once

they were out on the sidewalk. "Now on to the feed store."

"Ugh," said Roque. "Do we have to? I mean, the saddle shop was one thing. I never met Tom before today. We didn't have any history together. But the feed store is something else entirely."

"Relax," said Susana. "Just do what I told you and you'll be fine. You've got this."

She had already filled Roque in on the names and backgrounds of some of the men he was likely to see at the feed store. The guy who manned the cash register was Jimmy Ray Boyd. He was a livestock judge for the Future Farmers of America and had an encyclopedic knowledge of animal ailments and how to treat them. The one who always had a toothpick in his mouth was Roy Davidge. He raised Charolais cattle on his place south of town. He could be abrasive, Susana said, but he took care of his own, and he knew cattle. Willis Clark, the one with the walrus mustache and bald head, was descended from one of the town's founders, and his herd of Herefords had a lineage as long as his own. Gene Harris was the newcomer of the bunch. He'd bought his land back in the seventies. He was tall and lean.

All four of them were in here today, hanging around the cash register. They turned as the door jingled open and Susana walked in.

A whole lot of small talk followed. She greeted them, and they greeted her, and they all talked about the storm. Everyone had to say how they'd managed while snowed in, and what property damage they'd suffered. After they'd finished telling their own snowstorm tales of woe, they started in on their family, friends and neighbors.

Roque was starting to wonder if Susana would ever get around to actually buying any feed, but he kept quiet, smiling and nodding every now and then like she'd told him to. Jimmy Ray kept glancing at him, and so did some of the others.

Finally, Jimmy Ray asked, "Well, what can I do for you today, Miss Susana?"

She told him how many bags of feed and square bales of hay she needed. "I also need some anxiety meds for one of the horses, and some dewormer," she said.

"All righty, then. If you want to drive your truck around to the back, we'll get the feed and hay loaded while you shop for the other things."

"I'll have my hired man move the truck," she said.

Jimmy Ray's eyebrows shot up. "Hired man?"

"That's right." Susana nodded in Roque's direction. "I think you've seen Roque before. He's working for me now."

Roque could feel the ripple of surprise go through the cash register crowd. Willis hooked his thumbs in his belt and cast his eyes over Roque.

"So you got yourself a hired man, huh?" he said. "What all is he going to do?"

"Feeding, fencing, clearing brush. He's already grubbed the mesquite and cactus out of five of my horse pens."

Willis nodded cautiously. "Huh. Well, I'm glad to hear things are coming along well enough for you to hire some help."

"Actually, it's a barter arrangement," Susana said. "Roque's boarding his horse at my place in exchange for twenty hours of work a week."

Gene leaned his hip against the counter and gave Roque a doubtful look. "You have a horse, do you?"

"Yes, sir," said Roque.

"You remember Cisco, that big bay that belonged to Henry Hager?" said Susana. "That's Roque's horse."

Roy shifted a toothpick from one side of his mouth to the other. "I seem to recollect hearing you say once that you were kin to Henry Hager," he said. He looked as if he didn't believe it.

"Yes, sir," said Roque. "He married my grandmother about twenty years ago."

"Oh, yeah. I remember that," said Willis. "Yankee woman. Henry met her on a cruise ship. Got married on the cruise ship, too, if I recall."

"That's right," said Roque. "It was quite a shock to the families—or to the Hagers, at least. I don't know that my family was all that surprised. My nonna was always a firecracker."

"So I heard," said Willis. "She died a few years after, didn't she?"

"Yes, sir, she did."

"I never saw her but a time or two, but Henry sure seemed taken with her."

Roy squinted at Roque. "Didn't Henry used to bring you here with him sometimes? I seem to recall a little dark-headed boy, all duded up in chaps and spurs."

Roque laughed. "Yes, sir, that was me. I did love those chaps. Granddad liked to spoil me. It was fun, but unfortunately it gave me a wrong idea about what real cowboys wear on a daily basis."

The men chuckled.

"Yep, you were a regular dude when you first showed back up in town," said Roy.

They all took turns teasing him about his chaps and spurs, but the teasing was good-natured now, and Roque laughed at himself along with the rest of them.

"Henry Hager was a good man and a good customer," said Jimmy Ray. "He came to this store every week to buy his feed."

"I remember," said Roque. "Didn't there used to be one of those low chest-style coolers in here? Granddad would always get me a Mexican Coke."

"It's still here," said Jimmy Ray. "Just moved around back."

He came out from behind the counter and led the way to the worn glass-topped cooler.

"Yup, that's it," said Roque. "Boy, does that bring back memories. You still have Mexican Coke in it, too."

"Go on and get you one," said Jimmy Ray. "On the house."

"Well, thank you, Jimmy Ray," said Roque.

He opened the cooler and took out one of the curved pale green glass bottles. It felt smaller in his hand than it used to. He popped the metal lid off with the opener on the cooler's side and took a long draw.

"Ah," he said. "I've missed this. There's nothing quite like a Mexican Coke."

"It's the fructose," said Gene. "They make 'em with fructose in Mexico. That's why they taste different from American Coke."

Willis folded his arms over his chest. "So you're going to work for Susana," he said.

"Yes, sir. I've got a lot to learn, and I guess she's a good one to teach me."

"She is that," said Roy. "She worked as a hired hand out at my place years ago, when she was just a young'un. She could outwork a man twice her size and get the orneriest horses to do anything she wanted."

They spent a few more minutes shooting the breeze. Susana told them how Roque had fixed the plumbing at her house, and they all eyed him with fresh respect. Then Jimmy Ray asked if Susana wanted to put Roque on her account so he could buy feed for her, and they set that up.

Back in the truck, after the feed and hay had been loaded and Susana's purchases paid for, Roque shut the door, turned to Susana and asked, "Did that go as well as I think it did?"

She gave him a radiant smile. "It went very well. I couldn't have asked for it to go better. You're doing a good job, Roque. Keep on doing what you're doing, and don't get cocky."

"Ha! Yeah, that's good advice. You know, for a minute back there, I was feeling so confident, so in the groove with all the yes, sir, and no, sir, that I came *this close* to saying I reckon instead of I guess."

Susana's eyes widened and she held a hand to her chest. "Don't do that."

"I won't. I remembered you said not to try to sound Southern, and… Well, I *reckon* you're right. You've been right about everything else so far."

Everywhere they went, the message was the same. *This is Roque. He works for me.* And everywhere they went, people responded. Their attitudes shifted. Roque could hear it in their voices and see it in their eyes. He was somebody now.

At Darcy's Hardware, they split up. Roque turned down the power tool aisle in search of chainsaw parts—

And there was Dirk.

His step-cousin had his back to him, but Roque knew him instantly by his voice and the set of his shoulders. For a minute, it was almost like Granddad himself was standing there.

Dirk was talking to the owner of the hardware store, who seemed to be explaining why he didn't have any plumbing supplies in stock. Roque could hear the edge of irritation in Dirk's voice.

Then Dirk turned around and saw Roque.

Dirk's face already looked angry, with the jaw clamped tight in that way Roque remembered. Now he stopped in his tracks, staring at Roque from down the aisle.

For a second, Roque didn't know what to say, but he was rarely at a loss for words for long.

"Hello, Dirk," he said.

Dirk gave him a quick tight nod. "Roque. How are you?"

"Hanging in there," said Roque. "You?"

"Can't complain."

Dirk didn't look inclined to say more, and Roque didn't want to push him. Better quit while he was ahead.

"Okay then," he said. "Take care."

"Yeah, you, too," said Dirk.

And then he was gone.

CHAPTER NINE

SUSANA FOUND HER fence clips and waited
for Roque at the cash register. Within a
couple of minutes, he was heading her
way with that long-legged stride of his,
holding his packages high in triumph.

"They had the carburetor rebuild kit in
stock, and a spare chain. I got you a file,
too, and a guide for holding the chain at
thirty degrees. I like to just eyeball the
angle when I sharpen them, but I figured
you'd want to do it by the book."

"Good call."

The sun was shining bright in a clear
sky when they walked out into the parking lot. Roque reached the truck first and
opened the passenger door for Susana. The
small act of chivalry seemed a little out of
place when they were both wearing cowboy work boots, but Susana liked it, and
she liked watching Roque cross back to

the driver's side door. He certainly was a handsome man, and in his new Ropers, with his hat set low on his forehead and that drover coat showing scuff marks and traces of mud, he was starting to have the look of a real cowboy.

"I saw Dirk," he said after getting in and shutting the door.

"What, just now? In the store? How'd it go?"

"All right, I think. I kept it quick. It was a *hello, how are you, goodbye* sort of thing. Humble and polite, like you said."

"Good. Give him his space, and let him come to you. Dirk's a proud man, and he took a hit financially from that whole Masterson Acres thing. The Hagers used to rent the Masterson land and run their cattle on it, and I know they offered to buy it more than once. It had to be a nasty shock when the Mastersons sold to developers instead."

He started the truck. "So where to now? Home?"

"Let's go to my parents' shop first. I want a little treat after all those days of being snowbound. Are you hungry?"

"Are you kidding? I'm always hungry."

The parking lot of the Czech bakery was packed, with a long line wrapped around to the back for the drive-through. Roque had to park on the street.

The second Susana walked through the glass door, the aroma of the place—an unmistakable blend of strong coffee, hot oil, pastry and spices—washed over her in a comforting wave. It was the aroma of thousands of mornings from childhood through her teen years, of rolling out kolache dough and spooning meat onto tortillas, of pouring water into the huge coffee urns, of the constant bustle and chatter of siblings and cousins and parents, of doing her homework at a freshly wiped and slightly damp booth while snacking on pastries and coffee heavily diluted with milk.

Her mother was working the counter today. She moved so fast that her hands were a blur, but she spotted Susana instantly and gave her a quick smile. Susana waved and got in line with Roque.

"Looks like the rest of the town wanted a little post-snowstorm treat, too," said Roque.

"We won't have long to wait," said Susana. "My sister Monika is working drive-through, and my brother David is manning the fryers, and some of my Diaz cousins are on tacos. Most of these orders will be to go, so we'll be able to sit down as soon as a booth opens up. That one in the corner looks like it'll be available soon."

"I hope so," said Roque. "I'm getting hungrier by the second."

Sure enough, they reached the counter within a few minutes. The top couple of layers of the Formica were worn through from decades of orders being pushed across its surface. Monika was always saying how shabby it looked and how they ought to replace it with granite or marble, and update the whole interior while they were at it, but her parents refused to hear of it and Susana thought they were right. The place had a nice retro vibe, with its aqua-and-white checkerboard floor tiles and hard plastic orange booths, and the signs of wear meant that the place had been in business a long time and was there to stay.

Susana's mom had her thick brown hair piled high on her head and held in place with a bejeweled hair clip. She wore a crisp white apron with aqua stripes and long dangly earrings. Her bright blue eyes lit up at the sight of her eldest daughter.

"Zuzanka! Good to see you, siska. What'll it be?"

"Hi, Mom. I'd like two kolaches, one with cream cheese and one with apricot, and a cup of coffee…and whatever Roque's having."

Her mother darted a glance from Susana to Roque and back again.

"Oh! Are you together?"

The last word was heavy with meaning.

"Roque's my new hired man," said Susana.

There wasn't time to say more, which was part of the reason Susana had waited until this very moment to tell her mother about her arrangement with Roque. She couldn't stop her mom from speculating, but having Roque there in person on a busy morning in the shop would at least cut down on the questions.

"How nice!" said her mom, in a tone that clearly meant they'd be talking about this again later. "And what would you like, Roque?"

"I'll have three chorizo kolaches, two persimmon kolaches, two barbacoa tacos and coffee. And this one's on me."

He had his wallet out and the bills peeled off before Susana could say anything.

"That corner booth's ready now," he said to her. "Go sit down and I'll get our coffee."

He joined her within a few minutes, carrying two steaming mugs. She took hers in her hands and held it to her face. It was still too hot to sip, but she inhaled deeply and felt the fragrant steam on her face.

"Mmm, I needed this. Coffee never tastes quite as good anywhere else."

"Yeah, I think it's those big urns they make it in. They get the water really hot. That fancy coffee shop stuff doesn't do anything for me. Give me a good old-fashioned cup of piping hot Joe in a nice thick stoneware mug like this one right here any day."

"Me, too. We sell espresso here, too, but I've always liked plain strong coffee best." She set her mug down. "I might as well apologize in advance for whatever my mom's going to say or hint whenever she makes it over here to sit down and chat. I don't think she'll actually evaluate you as husband material out loud and to your face, but that'll be the direction her thoughts are going."

Roque gave Susana a sly smile and leaned across the table to say quietly, "Well, look at it this way. As long as she thinks there's a possibility of something happening between you and me, she won't try to set you up with any promising young men."

A shiver ran through her. Roque was practically whispering in her ear, and his curls were brushing her forehead. She'd been telling herself for a while now that she was too busy for dating, and that she was perfectly fine with that. But that wasn't exactly true. Lack of time wasn't the real issue behind her nonexistent romantic life. And Roque could make a girl change her mind. Those twinkling brown eyes, that broad span of shoulders, that devastating smile...

"Good point," she whispered back. It

would be no hardship to pretend to be involved with him.

Just then, Susana's mother set their order on the table and slid onto the seat beside Susana.

"Here's your food, siska. And before you go, I've got a bag of yesterday's pastries to send home with you. Maybe you and Roque can divide them up."

"Thanks, Mom."

"Yeah, thanks, Mrs. Vrba. Your pastries are a bright spot in my bachelor diet."

Susana's mom beamed at him. "Oh, you're so sweet. And call me Kristyna."

She turned back to Susana. "So how was your Christmas? I wish you could have been with us. Did you have enough to eat?"

"More than enough." Susana shot Roque a conspiratorial glance. "Roque helped me polish it off, as a matter of fact."

"Did he? Well! It's a good thing I brought so much food for you, then."

"It was delicious, too!" said Roque. "Those noodles! That sausage! And the pickled beets!"

Susana thought Roque was laying it on

a bit thick. She had a hard time believing anyone actually liked pickled beets. But her mother ate up the praise.

"If you like noodles," she said, "you should come to the Chili Noodle Soup Supper. Only a month away!"

"What is the Chili Noodle Soup Supper?" asked Roque. "Do you really put noodles in the chili? That sounds kind of radical."

Susana's mother laughed. "No, no. Separate dishes. The menu is chili, chicken noodle soup, chicken salad sandwiches, homemade bread and kolaches."

"Ooh!" said Roque. "And where is this amazing event held?"

"In Novak, where Susana's grandparents live. It's a fundraiser for the church, open to the community, held every February. Bring Roque to the supper, Zuzanka. Bring him to the prep day, too, and the noodle-making day."

"I wish I could, Mom, but that's a lot of days. You know I can't leave the horses for that long."

"Well, come to the supper, then. Both of you."

"We'll do our best," said Roque.

"Okay." Kristyna looked at Susana. "So! Roque is your hired man now."

"That's right. It's a barter arrangement—twenty hours of work a week in exchange for board for his horse."

"Good! It must be nice, having a big strong man on the place."

"It's pretty convenient, all right," said Susana, thinking of those fifty-pound feed bags.

"I try to pull my weight," said Roque. "But I gotta say, Susana's a real powerhouse. She may be small, but she's strong. It's all I can do just to keep up with her."

"She was always a hard worker, and so determined." Kristyna got up. "All right. I'll let you eat now. Don't forget to pick up those pastries when you go."

"I won't. Thanks, Mom."

"Thank you, Kristyna!" Roque said sweetly.

When they were alone again, Susana rolled her eyes at him.

"What?" he said as he picked up his first taco.

"I notice you didn't need me to coach

you on how to charm my mother. You did just fine with that on your own."

"Yeah, well, she was always nice to me. That's why I like this place so much. I never felt like an outsider here. Not to mention the food! These chorizo kolaches are so good!"

"Those aren't real kolaches, you know. Real kolaches have fruit or cream cheese, not Mexican sausage."

"I don't care. I love them anyway."

Roque had just finished his tacos and was started on his kolaches when a big bald man with a handlebar mustache swooped in on them with a loud, friendly roar.

"Hey, Bobby Six-Guns! How you doing?"

"Hey there, Mr. Mendoza. Good to see you. You know Susana, right?"

"Sure! We're almost related, aren't we, Susana?" He turned back to Roque. "I haven't seen your horse on the property for a while. Is he okay?"

"Oh, yeah, he's great. I'm just board-ing him out at Susana's place now, in ex-change for twenty hours of work a week."

"Ooooohhhh," Mr. Mendoza said in an

isn't-that-interesting tone, looking rapidly back and forth between them. "Well, that explains that. So I guess that means you're not going to need to rent my place anymore, huh?"

"Actually, I'd very much like to go on living there."

Mr. Mendoza cocked his head and squinted at him. "Really? Very much? You'd very much like to go on living in my old horse trailer?"

"That was the deal we made."

"Yeah, but I'd have thought you'd be sick of that by now."

Roque shrugged. "I'm a simple man, Mr. Mendoza. As long as I have a warm, dry place to lay my head at night, I'm good."

Mr. Mendoza gave him a shrewd look. "You mean you can't afford anything better right now."

"That, too."

"Well, I can understand that. But I feel bad charging you rent just for that old trailer. The price we agreed on included pasturing the horse there."

"True, but the price was plenty low to begin with."

Mr. Mendoza rubbed his chin, then said, "You know what? You been a good tenant to me, and since you're open to a work barter situation, how 'bout if you just clear the brush from around the foundation of the house, and pay the electric bill, and we'll call it good for the rest of the year? Actually, hold on. The rest of the year is only, like, three days. We'll call it good for the rest of this year and next year."

"Whoa, seriously? Thank you. That's very generous, Mr. Mendoza."

Mr. Mendoza waved this off. "Ah, don't mention it. That lot wasn't doing anybody any good just sitting there. And honestly, I'm glad to have you on the place. With that big metal barn, I was always worried about vandals and partying teenagers and stuff. Having you there is an extra layer of security. And if you leave it in better shape than you found it, I'll be more than satisfied."

They shook hands on the deal, and Mr. Mendoza picked up his order and left.

"Well, how about that?" said Roque. "Things are looking up for me all over."

Susana smiled at him. "I told you they would."

"You did. You're very wise."

Just then, Susana's phone went off. The caller was already in her contacts. It was Roy Davidge.

She answered.

"Hello, Roy. What can I do for you?"

"Well," said Roy, "I got a widowed sister that was hard hit by the snowstorm. She's been without water for about a week now, and none of the plumbers will call her back. So I was wondering if you'd be willing to lend out that hired man of yours to do some plumbing repairs."

"I think that could be arranged," Susana said. "How about if I put him on the line with you right now?"

As she handed the phone to Roque, she felt a warm glow of satisfaction. It was official. Their trip to town was an unqualified success.

CHAPTER TEN

FIXING THE PLUMBING at Roy's sister's house took Roque the rest of the day. She sent him home with two quarts of home-canned beef stew and a bottle of home-made wine.

Early the next morning, he showed up at Susana's place in time for morning feeding. By now he was getting to know the routine pretty well. After the horses were fed, he went to work rebuilding the carburetor on the chainsaw. Before long, he had it running and was ready to start on that big mesquite stump in the back of the pen.

It was a big job, but fun. It felt good to tax his muscles in the winter morning and work up an honest sweat, and make slow but steady headway against that old monstrosity of a stump. Little by little, he dug it out, cut away its roots and dug some more, finally exposing enough of it to wrap it up in a chain. Then he secured the chain to Susana's tractor and started the engine.

He could feel the resistance in the dense network of tough spreading roots. But Susana had run the hose overnight to soften the soil, and finally the old stump gave up its hold and ripped free of the ground.

He called Susana over to see. The two of them stood side by side, gloating over the gaping hole the stump had left behind.

"It's a beautiful day," said Roque. "After I finish up here, how's about we get started on those trails?"

Susana shook her head. "I don't want you to go over on your hours. You've already been working since… Hold on a minute." She checked her phone. "Roque! You've already gone over. You've worked twenty-two hours this week."

He shrugged. "I don't mind. I'm not tired, and I've got nothing else to do until Zac calls me in for work again. Let's get going on those trails. We can make a start, at least."

"No. I'm not going to overwork you. I can't have you burning out."

"Oh, come on! The chainsaw's running

great and the weather's fantastic. Why not take advantage of all that while we can?"

"I'm sorry, Roque. I appreciate your enthusiasm, I really do, but our agreement was for twenty hours a week."

"Well, I can't just leave this giant pit in the pen," Roque said. "I've got to at least fill it in and grade it and take the stump to the burn pile."

She shot him a look. "I do know how to operate the tractor myself, you know. I'll take care of it. You head home and I'll see you next week."

He tried another tack. "Please don't send me home. I've got nothing to do there but lie on my bunk and stare up at the ceiling."

She turned those clear blue eyes on him. She had the sweetest face he'd ever seen. And she was weakening; he could tell. It really was a beautiful day, with a clear sky and not a breath of wind.

"How about this?" she said. "How about if you and I go for a ride?"

He wasn't expecting that. "Seriously?"

"Sure. Thanks to you, I'm actually caught up on my own work for a change, and you haven't even seen the rest of the property. Let's saddle up Cisco and Leda and go."

SUSANA WAS TAKING Leda's saddle out of the barn when her text tone went off. She draped the saddle over the fence and checked her phone.

The message was from her sister Monika.

I hear Bobby Six-Guns is working for you now.

Susana typed her reply. His name is Roque, and he's actually a pretty good guy.

Well, he sure is cute, Monika answered. Maybe there's a little workplace romance in your future? Or in your present??

Susana made an indignant sound. Roque, who was securing Cisco's lead rope to the fence six feet off, glanced her way.

"What's the matter?" he asked.

"Nothing," said Susana.

She typed, Workplace romances aren't a good idea. Roque and I have already talked it over and agreed to keep things professional.

Monika's next text arrived as Susana was tightening Leda's cinch.

If you say so.

"I do say so," Susana muttered. "That's why I said so."

"What was that?" Roque asked.

"Nothing," Susana said again.

She put her phone away in her saddlebag, picked up the currycomb and started working it over Leda's coat in small circular motions. Roque was doing the same thing with Cisco, making soft crooning noises under his breath, a faint smile at the corners of his lips. His long strong hands smoothed the bay's glossy coat with an expert touch. He'd rolled up his shirt sleeves, revealing a network of deep scratches on his forearms and hands from cactus spines and mesquite thorns.

So, Monika thought Roque was cute. Of course she did. Who wouldn't? Tall and strong, with that head of thick curls, that teasing smile, those laughing dark eyes…

"What are you looking at?" Roque asked.

Susana gave herself a shake. What *was* she looking at?

She pointed at the scratches on his forearms. "You look as if you've been fighting a bobcat," she said.

He chuckled. "Well, you know what they say. What doesn't kill you makes you stronger."

"Yeah, I don't know that I believe that. Sometimes what doesn't kill you leaves you maimed and…"

"Scarred?" asked Roque. "Yeah. But scars can be useful. They remind you not to make the same mistakes again."

He met her gaze over Cisco's back, his dark eyes more serious than she'd ever seen them before.

"I take it we're talking about metaphorical scars now," she said. "Are you thinking of that ex-girlfriend you mentioned?"

"Layla, yeah. Even when we were together, I knew she was no good for me, but once she wasn't there anymore, it was like the whole world fell apart. You know how it is."

"Not really," she said. "Most of my romantic relationships have fizzled out before they really started."

"I find that hard to believe," he said. "A pretty woman like you, and sweet and kind, too? You must get asked out plenty."

"Oh, I've had my share of first dates. Second and third dates, not so much. My very first date ever sort of set the tone. Homecoming, junior year. My date came to the house, gave me the corsage, my mom took way too many pictures. Nice boy, good-looking, very polite. Then on the way to the dance, I saw a dog wandering around—dirty, painfully thin, no collar. Well, of course we had to stop and check on it. The dog had a nasty cut on her leg, and her teats were engorged, so there were puppies. We hunted for the puppies, found them, took them back to my house. They were shepherd mix, really cute and only a few days old. By the time I'd treated the mother dog's hurt leg, and had her and the pups settled in the corner of the room I shared with my sisters, it was too late for the dance, and my date had had enough. He never called me again. Started dating a friend of mine not long after. And ever since then, it's been a recurring theme in my romantic life—a stray dog, a sick horse, a rescue that needs to be picked up somewhere, a fence that needs mending. Always something."

"Well, the right guy wouldn't be put off by all that. He'd stay with you, and help you take care of that horse or mend that fence. Order a pizza."

"I agree. But it hasn't happened yet. They've all pretty much run away screaming."

"You just need to find a country boy. Someone who's used to animals and fences and things."

"I thought the same thing for a while. Unfortunately, those guys tend to have places of their own. They like my work ethic and knowledge base, but they expect me to put those things to use on their properties. My place is baggage they want no part of."

Roque shook his head. "That isn't fair."

"No. But it's the way things are. And I'm not in a position to bargain."

"What do you mean?"

"I'm not…" She sighed, struggling to

find the right words. "I tend to be the friend or the sister of the girls the guys are really interested in, not the main attraction. I always feel like I'm expected to be grateful that a guy agreed to take me out at all."

Roque looked outraged. "Why would you think that?"

She shrugged. "The guy that asked me to homecoming? After I loaded that dirty dog and her puppies into his nice freshly vacuumed car, I remember him staring at me as I sat there in my dress covered with dog hair, with this look on his face that said, *You aren't worth this*."

Roque didn't answer.

"And it always seems to come back to that," Susana went on. "So I told my family not to set me up anymore. I told them I didn't have time for dating, but that's just an excuse. The truth is, I can't go through it anymore, getting my hopes up and having them crushed. I'm going to end up alone with my animals anyway, so I might as well skip the raised expectations and effort and drama, and go straight to that part. It's better that way. More peaceful.

And if it's also a little lonely at times, then that's just the price I have to pay."

Roque set down the currycomb, walked over to her and took her shoulders in his hands.

"You listen to me, Susana. You are a beautiful woman—and generous and hard-working and kind. You're the whole package."

His gaze was burning into her. She shook her head and looked down, but he gently lifted her chin. "I mean it. The right guy is going to take one look at you and know he's struck gold. He's not going to be scared off by all this that you do. He's going to see it for what it is, an adventure, and he'll want to be right there with you for the ride. He's going to hold on to you and never let go."

Her heart was pounding itself sore in her chest. He was so near, crouching a little to bring his face close to hers. His hands on her shoulders, the furrow in his brow, the grim set of his mouth with no trace of its usual teasing smile—he was all she could see, the whole world.

She knew she ought to say something, but

her mind had been wiped clean of words. She couldn't think of anything but Roque.

His hands tightened their grip on her shoulders. Just for a second, he moved a tiny bit closer to her. Then he straightened, gave her a quick nod and patted her shoulder.

"So don't you forget it," he said.

He picked up his currycomb and went back to grooming Cisco. His back was to her now, which was a good thing because she was pretty sure her feelings were plainly written on her face. She didn't know where to look or what to do.

Then Leda let out an exasperated whuffle. Susana turned around and went back to the familiar routine of preparing for a ride. By the time she got Leda saddled, she'd regained some semblance of calm.

Roque tightened Cisco's cinch and gave Susana a quick smile over the horse's back.

"Ready?" he asked.

"Ready," she said.

SUSANA COULDN'T REMEMBER the last time she'd ridden for pleasure—and riding with Roque was definitely a pleasure. He had

the seat of an experienced horseman, relaxed and easy, core engaged, legs and
hips softly flowing in response to Cisco's
movements.

They went down the lane between the
pens all the way to the end of the cleared
land, then followed the remains of an old
cattle trail through some light brush. The
last of snow had melted away. The only
evidence of the Extreme Winter Weather
Event was in the soggy, slimy, frozen and
thawed herbage, and in the live oaks, which
ordinarily kept their dark green leaves
through the winter, not shedding them until
new growth came in to take their place, but
were now covered with dead brown foliage.

She showed Roque how far her property went. There was some flatter land
that would do well for additional horse
pens, and a gently rolling wooded area
where the trails would go.

"Eventually, I'd like to have three or four
separate trails," she said. "There's plenty of
space for that many if they curve around
enough. A winding trail is what you want,
but not too winding. You want the riders
to wonder what's around the next bend,

but not get worn out from all the twisting and turning. Then every so often, the trail should break out from the tree cover into an open area. Some variation in slope is good, but again, not too much—though it might be good to have at least one trail that's more difficult than the rest, to provide a challenge for more experienced riders. Each trail ought to take about an hour to complete at walking pace. There's a nice bluff that would make a good spot to stop and rest awhile and take some pictures at around the halfway point."

"That low area down there would make a good open space," said Roque, pointing. "It just needs a few of the mesquites and cedars grubbed out."

"I think so, too. I'd like to grow hay there. A hay field is always pretty to look at. Plus I'd have the hay—enough for my own needs and extra to sell in a good year."

"Ooh, a side hustle! Good thinking. So how do you actually put in the trails? What's the process?"

"Well, first you walk through with a chainsaw. Find the natural openings between the trees and make them wider. Cut back the limbs in a space as wide as a dozer, about six feet. Anything to be dozed gets cut off at waist height, but if it's small enough, you can go ahead and trim it down to ground level. You don't want to leave any stumps to trip the horses or grow back later. Once you've finished the first pass, you come back with the dozer and clear it all away."

Roque nodded. "So when do we get started?"

She thought a moment. "Not until we're sure we're ready to follow through. I don't want to get started and then have to stop and watch it all grow back again."

"How about Monday?" he asked. "New Year's Day."

"Okay," she said. "Monday it is."

Then they had to figure out where the first trail should start. They finally settled on an opening between two pecan trees whose branches met overhead in an arch. One of the trees had a heart-shaped hollow where a limb had fallen away.

"We can call it the Sweetheart Trail," Roque said.

Susana stuffed some alfalfa hay into the rack at the top of the feeder, then poured the sweet-smelling pellets into the trough. Amadeus and Damascus dug in.

The sun was on its way down, but she lingered a moment, relishing the sight. No more cockleburs in Damascus's flaxen mane and tail, no more pieces of jumping cactus on Amadeus's dun coat. Behind them, their pasture stretched out smooth and clear—a little bare and brown in spots, especially where the big mesquite stump had been, but it would all grass over soon enough.

And early tomorrow, just after morning feeding, she and Roque would start making the first trail.

A thrill of excitement shot through her at the thought. They'd start at the sweetheart tree, plotting the course of the trail and making the first pass with the chainsaw. It was impossible to estimate how long it would take to actually finish the job. But she'd seen Roque handling the big chainsaw as easily as if it was a leaf blower, and every task she'd given him had been completed faster than she'd expected.

If she was honest with herself, her excitement was about more than the trail itself as a finished product. She was looking forward to the process as much as the result. It wasn't often that the two of them worked so closely together. Usually she had him clearing land, mending fence or feeding horses by himself, while she taught a riding lesson or did groundwork or something. But this would be a full day spent in each other's company.

Her mind kept coming back to that near kiss, the day they'd gone riding together, and all the things he'd said to her then—how the right guy wouldn't be put off by her work but would embrace it. He'd had very definite ideas about this right guy, whoever he was.

He'd even said she was beautiful.

She felt her cheeks heating up and tried to put the memory out of her mind. Roque was a good worker and a good friend. She didn't want to ruin what they had by trying to turn it into something different. And yet…she was ninety-five percent sure that he'd wanted to kiss her that day, and ninety-nine percent sure that she'd wanted him to.

She was just setting the empty buckets back in the truck when her phone started playing "A Country Boy Can Survive"—Roque's ringtone. She smiled. She'd always liked Hank Jr., but now she never heard him without also hearing Roque's Jersey-accented voice singing along.

"Hey there," she said. "I hope you're about to get a good night's sleep, because we're starting the trail bright and early tomorrow."

"Yeah, about that…"

His voice trailed away. A lead pit formed in her stomach.

"One of Zac's subcontractors had to reschedule," Roque went on. "That means Zac had to shuffle some other things around. He wants me with him tomorrow, framing a new garage in Schraeder Lake."

"Oh," Susana said. She could hear the disappointment in her own voice.

"I'm really sorry. I'd get out of it if I could. But—"

"No, no," she said. "I understand. This

is your day job. You can't skip out on it to come work for me."

"But you and I have an agreement, too, and I don't want to give you short shrift. How about if I come Tuesday instead?"

"No, Tuesday's my lesson day. I'm booked solid."

"Oh, right. Well then, how 'bout Wednesday?"

"Wednesday works for me."

"Okay. I'll see you then."

But on Wednesday, it rained all day. And on Thursday, Roque got called in to work for Zac again, on a bathroom remodel that was estimated to take two days.

"I don't know what the deal is," he said over the phone Wednesday evening. "Until now it's been like pulling teeth to get enough hours to pay my bills. Now, suddenly, Zac's giving me all the hours I can handle."

"It's all right," Susana said. "We'll try again next week."

He let out a frustrated sigh. "I'm sorry. I feel like I'm letting you down."

"Don't feel that way. We knew all along that we'd have to be flexible with your schedule. There's still time in the week for you to get your twenty hours in."

"But not to start on the trails. We have to both be available at the same time for that."

She forced herself to sound cheerful. "Look, as long as you give me twenty hours a week, I'm happy."

But she didn't feel happy at all.

Susana had just finished Friday's morning feeding when Pirko gave a sharp bark and ran toward the driveway. There was Roque's truck, turning in from the road, just like on that first day.

A thrill of pleasure shot through her, so sharp it almost hurt. He was here! She wanted to run to him, just like Pirko, but she made herself keep to a sedate pace.

As he got out of the truck, she called out, "I thought you had to work for Zac."

Roque hurried toward her, grinning from ear to ear. "The plumbers got delayed because their materials didn't come in. Everything's still in short supply because of the snowstorm. Bad news for the homeowners, but good news for you and me. I'm free today and tomorrow, and there's no rain in the forecast. Let's get going! I have a lot of hours to make up."

He was bursting with energy and excitement, as if he'd been given an unexpected holiday. Susana felt the same way. She did a quick mental reshuffling of her day's plans.

"We'll take the four-wheeler to the trail head," she said. "Easier than lugging the tools by hand, and the four-wheeler can go places the truck can't."

They loaded the chainsaw onto the four-wheeler's cargo bin, along with some loppers and a bow saw.

"Granddad used to have one of these," Roque said. "I loved driving that thing."

"Is that a hint that you'd like to drive this one?"

He shrugged. "I wouldn't say no if you offered."

"Go ahead. It makes more sense for you to hold on to the controls and me to hold on to you. If you hold on to me and we hit a bump, we'd both go flying off."

He nodded sagely. "Sure, that's the reason."

He flung a long leg effortlessly over the seat of the four-wheeler, took hold of the handlebars and gave her a devilish grin.

"Born to ride, baby," he said.

She laughed and got on. It wasn't as easy for her, and her legs looked childishly small against his. She put her arms around his waist. His abs were flat and rock-hard.

He laid an enormous hand over both of hers and gave them a quick squeeze—probably just making sure she had a good grip, but she liked the feel of it.

"Hold on tight," he said, then started the engine and took off.

She laid her cheek against his back and watched as the horse pens gave way to scrub and then woods. The ride was bumpy enough to justify the firm hold she was keeping on him.

Too soon, the four-wheeler slowed and stopped, and the engine cut off.

"Here we are," Roque said. "Head of the trail."

The interlocking limbs of the two pecan trees met over their heads. Some of last year's pecan husks still clung to the branches, burst into star shapes. A strand of ivy curved under the heart-shaped hollow, its leaves making heart shapes of their own.

Susana climbed off the four-wheeler, letting her hand linger on Roque's back a second longer than she needed to, and took the loppers out of the cargo bin. Roque picked up the chainsaw and they started walking the trail.

The rain had washed the woods bright and clean, turning the lichens into lime-colored splashes against the dark trunks, and making every bare twig end stand out sharp and clear. The woods were mostly oaks and elms, with a few dark green cedars. Some of the post oaks still clung to the last of their bronzy leaves. The slender gray branches of possumhaw holly were bare except for clusters of red berries.

"Some of these are red oaks," she said. "They'll be gorgeous in the fall. So will the elms. And in the spring, we'll have dogwoods and redbuds blooming in the understory."

It was easy to fall into the habit of speaking in plurals—we, us, ours.

"I think it's pretty nice right now," said Roque.

They picked their way forward in fits and starts. Sometimes the right path was obvious; sometimes they had to stop and think and hash it out. The very act of talking it over with Roque made everything clearer, and in the end, they always found a route that they agreed was best. She'd forgotten how helpful it could be to have another person, not just as a sounding board, but with good ideas of his own to contribute. She'd been working alone for a long time now.

Once they knew where they were going, Roque would start clearing the path with the chainsaw. Occasionally Susana would clip something with the loppers, but mostly she moved branches out of the way after Roque cut them. The trail felt snugly enclosed, with all the branches crossing overhead. A mated pair of cardinals kept them company, flitting around and eating dusty blue juniper berries. Sometimes they saw deer tracks. Pirko scampered around, sniffing everything.

She and Roque were walking side by

side, feeling out the next stretch of trail, when Roque suddenly halted and put out an arm in front of her.

"What's wrong?" she asked.

"Snake," he said.

"Where?"

He pointed. A mass of coils, sandy-colored with patches of black-and-white, lay in a patch of sunlight on a rock.

His arm still barred her way, as if it could protect her. She gently pushed it down and stepped forward to take a closer look.

"It's just a hognose," she said. "He won't hurt anyone."

"Are you sure? Looks like a rattler to me."

"The coloring is similar. But see how his snout turns up?"

Just then, Pirko noticed the snake. She jumped straight up in the air and let loose with her alarm bark. The snake raised its head, hissed and spread its hood, like a cobra.

"Hush, Pirko," Susana said. "Leave the snake alone."

Pirko backed up, giving a few parting barks, until she was hidden behind Roque.

Roque bent down and rubbed Pirko behind the ears. "You're sure that isn't a dangerous snake?" he asked.

"Positive. Hognoses are good snakes. They eat vermin."

"But are there rattlers and things around here?"

"Oh, sure. Rattlers, coral snakes, copperheads and water moccasins. We've got 'em all."

Roque took a furtive look around as if expecting them all to come slithering out at once.

"Are you scared?" Susana asked.

His gaze came to rest on her, the apprehension in his eyes slowly giving way to shock as he realized she was teasing him—shock, and pleasure.

"No," he said, scowling. "Not much."

She patted him on the arm. "Don't worry, Roque. I won't let the scary snakes hurt you."

He grinned and made a feint at her, as if he was going to tickle her, but pulled back at the last second. What was happening here? Were they flirting? It had been so long since Susana flirted that she wasn't sure if this qualified. But whatever it was, it felt good.

ROQUE AND SUSANA spent most of January doing the chainsaw work on the Sweetheart Trail. It was the most fun Roque had had in years.

His height and muscle mass made things possible for him that simply weren't for Susana—operating the chainsaw, reaching high limbs. Just being around her made him feel gigantic. But she could work as long and hard as he could. It didn't seem possible for there to be so much strength in so small a package.

He didn't want to quit at the end of the day, and the first thing he thought of in the morning was getting back to work on it. And in between, he dreamed about it.

Susana showed up in a few of his dreams as well. That small womanly figure of hers, moving between the trees, reaching up to clip a stray branch, dragging the cut limbs out of the way. The way her blue eyes lit up when she got excited. How it felt to make her laugh. It had been a long time since he'd actually enjoyed a woman's company. Those last months with Layla had been pretty heavy going.

But Susana was nothing like Layla.

There was a sweetness about her, a kind of wholeheartedness, that he'd never seen or imagined in Layla, or in any other woman he'd ever known. He couldn't just rush in like he usually did, though. If he was going to…pursue her, he'd have to tread lightly and take things slow. Heck, she'd written a whole paragraph about keeping things professional between them, and put it in that contract of hers, which he'd signed of his own free will. Since then, there'd been more than a few times when he'd been almost certain that her feelings for him went well beyond professional, contract or no contract. But he couldn't assume she was ready to throw caution to the wind just because he was. This was one relationship he couldn't afford to mess up.

CHAPTER ELEVEN

ONE OF THE best things about having Roque around, work-wise, was being able to send him to town to pick up feed and run errands. Going to town was always such a time suck. Before Roque came along, Susana had done her best to organize her town trips for maximum efficiency, but sending him in her place was even better.

The problem was that he always came back with more than she'd asked for. She'd send him to the lumberyard for fencing supplies, and he'd come back with new clients. Which was a good thing, obviously. Susana wasn't petty enough to mind the slight disruption to her routine when it meant more business. She liked knowing what to expect and having time to prepare mentally to meet new people, but she could adapt.

In fact, the most unsettling thing about

Roque's unpredictability was that she was starting to like it. Once in a while, she actually found herself looking forward to the next surprise. Before he'd come along, she'd been content enough to follow her routine. Now…things were different. *She* was different. And change meant risk.

A few days after lining up the new clients, Roque went to town to get some more fuel-to-oil mix for the chainsaw, in preparation for what Susana hoped would be their final push on the trail. The dozer work ought to go quicker than the chainsaw work. The end was in sight at last.

Her first clue that her plans might go sideways was when Roque texted to ask if she wanted any food from Lalo's Kitchen.

Thanks, but I already ate, she'd typed, then added, Don't forget our plans.

I won't, came his reply, followed by several seconds of dancing dots, and then the words, Hey, how come there's no chainsaw emoji?

She'd smiled, then told him, Never mind that. There's a real chainsaw waiting at home with your name written all over it.

Too late, she realized she'd referred to

the equine center as his home. But he just replied, I know. I'll be back soon, and we'll finish the trail.

Susana slid her phone into her back pocket. Had she grown too unguarded with Roque? He was more than a hired man, more than a friend. Her mind returned, as it so often did these days, to that near-kiss several weeks ago, when they'd first gone riding together. Ever since then, there'd been plenty of conversation and friendliness between them, but nothing else. Roque had been a perfect gentleman.

She appreciated his restraint. After all, they'd agreed to keep things between them on a nonromantic footing, even signed a contract to that effect. But maybe self-control had nothing to do with it. Maybe he just wasn't interested. Maybe she'd been wrong, and he hadn't wanted to kiss her at all that day.

The thought was oddly depressing. Why should it bother her to think Roque might not be attracted to her? That was what she wanted, wasn't it? She'd hired him to do a job in exchange for fair compensation. And he did that job well. *Very* well. Better than expected. The fact that he was fun to be around, and good to look at, was extraneous to the main point.

His social standing in the community had certainly gone up in the past month. He'd given Susana the credit for that—which was fair, to a point. Once they'd let people know he was working for her, and he'd taken her advice about how to present himself, he'd grown a lot more popular. But she'd only taken away the impediments so everyone could see him for who he really was—a friendly, lively, warmhearted guy who loved country life and was truly interested in other people.

She gave her head a hard shake. *Stop it. Don't mess up a good thing by trying to turn it into something else.*

Her phone dinged with a new text.

Going to be a little late. Will be in touch.

She let out an exasperated sigh. He'd be in touch? What was that supposed to mean? She didn't want him in touch. She wanted him here, where he'd said he'd be.

In a way, her irritation was a relief. Yes,

Roque was a great guy, but also about as different from her temperamentally as possible. She needed to keep that in mind.

She might as well get to work on the pen for Rufus and Theophilus, the new horses that would be arriving at the end of the week. Roque had already cleared the scrub and set the T-posts. Now Susana just needed to run the fencing and hang the gate. She went to it, making a mental note to get a new feeder and water trough from town before the week was out.

Half an hour later, Roque still hadn't arrived, and Susana's irritation had gone up a notch. She had just pulled out her phone to ask him for a status update when his ringtone went off for FaceTime.

Now what? She pressed the green button, and there was Roque's grinning face, bursting with excitement.

"Hey," she said. "Where are you? We said we were going to finish the chainsaw work today."

"I know. I'm sorry. But I have a good reason. I've got something to show you. What do you say to this?"

His face vanished, the screen jostled and suddenly she was looking at...

A big piece of machinery, with several rollers inside a track, a scoop-shaped blade in front and a seat perched up on top. Its outline was blurred by all the scrub and dead weed stalks surrounding it.

"What is that?" she asked, though she already knew.

"It's a dozer," he said. "It's been sitting in this guy's field for two years."

"Okaaaayyy," she said. "So what does that have to do with us?"

Roque's face appeared in the screen again. "Well, see, I went to pick up some lunch at Lalo's Kitchen and Mr. Mendoza was there getting a beer. And we got to talking about the trail work out at your place and how much progress we'd made, and how pretty soon we were going to need a dozer. And he said, speaking of dozers, some guy had just offered him an old one pretty cheap. The only catch is, it isn't running."

"That's a catch, all right," Susana said. She could see where this was going.

"Yeah, well, it's fixable if you know

what you're doing," Roque went on. "Mr. Mendoza could get it running again if he tried, but he already has his own equipment, so it isn't really worth his while. But he said maybe I ought to go take a look, and I said sure. So Mr. Mendoza called the guy and gave him my number, and the guy called me, and I drove out."

"Okay," said Susana. "So what's wrong with it?"

"Oh, there's no telling," Roque said cheerfully. "Between the rust and the dirt dauber nests, probably a lot more than when the guy first parked it in the field. The tracks and rollers are in pretty good shape, but there are rat droppings under the seat and an old bird's nest perched over the lift cylinder. But I can get it running again. Once we get it to your place, I'll open it up, take it apart and see what's what. It might need nothing more than for me to drain the old fuel and replace the fuel lines and filters."

And it might need a whole lot more. Susana's mind was suddenly filled with images of dollar signs.

"Do you have any experience with dozer repair?" she asked.

"No, but I've worked on plenty of diesel engines before. How hard can it be? Ultimately, I figure a fuel pump is a fuel pump and air filters are air filters. I can sort it out."

His breezy confidence was so appealing. Susana wanted to give in to it. But what if she plunked down the cash for this rusted-out hulk, and fronted the money for all these fuel pumps and such, and the thing still didn't run?

"I don't know, Roque. It could turn out to be a good deal, but it could also turn into a huge waste of time and money."

"Hold on," said Roque. "You haven't heard the best part. I already talked the guy down from his original price. I gave him the whole spiel about how it might cost more than it's worth to repair, yada yada. We went back and forth for a while, and when the dust settled, he said he'd be willing to work a trade. We can take the dozer in exchange for some riding lessons for his kid."

"How old a kid?"

"Thirteen. A daughter. He just got custody after not seeing her for eight years, and it sounds like he's not sure what to do with her now that he's got her."

"How many lessons?"

"Two a week for three months."

"Whoa! That seems a little steep for a piece of machinery that isn't even running."

"Well, the thing is, we need to offer him that much just to match what he'd get for selling it for scrap metal."

"It sounds like we might end up selling it for scrap metal ourselves, after spending a whole lot of time and energy and money trying to fix it."

"But we know we need a dozer to finish the trails. We can either pay to rent one, in which case we spend money and have to give the dozer back when we're done, or pay to fix this one, in which case we still have the dozer at the end of the job. Heck, once we're finished using it, you could probably sell it for more than we put into it."

"You don't know that. If we rent a dozer, we'll at least be getting one that actually runs, and we won't have to do all this extra labor that still won't guarantee that we have a working dozer at the end of it."

"I can get it running," Roque said.

The light of conviction in his voice was irresistible. His eyes shone with certainty. Susana wavered and finally said, "Okay."

His grin split his face. "Yesss! You won't regret this. I'm going to get a new battery installed right now so me and the guy can load the dozer onto Mr. Mendoza's flatbed trailer and bring it home."

"Is Mr. Mendoza there with you? I thought he just made the introductions."

"Yeah, well, he couldn't resist coming out to take a look. Professional interest, you know."

In other words, an excuse to stand around looking under the hood of an engine.

"He's been keeping the guy occupied for me so I could talk it over with you," Roque went on.

"Does this guy have a name?" Susana asked.

"Kevin Fox. He lives in that place behind the old water tower with all the machinery in the yard."

"Yeah, I know it. Well, you'd better bring this Kevin with you. We need to make a contract for the trade and figure out lesson times that work for all of us. Is the daughter there?"

"Yeah, she's here. You want I should bring her, too?"

"Might as well. The more the merrier." It was pretty clear that they weren't going to get any chainsaw work done today anyhow.

So they all came—Kevin Fox, his daughter Gillian, Mr. Mendoza and Roque. Pirko was delighted to have so many visitors on the place at once. She kept darting from one to the other for pets.

Kevin looked pretty young to be the father of a thirteen-year-old. He was skinny and unkempt, with longish hair standing up all over his head, and seemed a little uneasy around his daughter, as if she were a bomb that might go off. Gillian didn't strike Susana as a very explosive person, though. She didn't have much to say for herself. She certainly didn't show any interest in the horses, though she did give Pirko a few furtive pats on the head. She seemed to be trying to hold herself as still as possible.

By the time the contract had been made and signed, and the dozer had been unloaded, and Gillian's lessons had been scheduled, and everyone had finished talking the whole thing over for the umpteenth time, and the Foxes and Mr. Mendoza had driven off, the sun was well on its way down. As Susana had predicted, the final stretch of chainsaw work would have to be postponed until another day.

THE DOZER WAS still sitting there, not running, when Gillian showed up for her first lesson the next day.

"Hi, Gillian!" Susana said. "Good to see you. We're going to get started right away, getting the horse out of his pen, and grooming and saddling him. While we do that, I'm going to go over some ground rules, and then we'll get you in the saddle. Are you ready?"

Gillian nodded.

Susana led her to Barrymore's pen. The chestnut gelding came right to the gate, looking eager and alert. Susana had decided to use him as Gillian's lesson horse because he had such beautiful manners. Whoever had trained him had done a great job, and it seemed a shame to keep him cooped up and let it all go to waste. Besides, part of her deal with his owner was that she would provide exercise for him, and she figured this qualified.

She kept up a stream of talk, going over the ground rules as they came up naturally—the importance of shutting gates, how to safely approach a horse, putting on the halter, how to butterfly the lead rope instead of wrapping it around your hand. She would demonstrate each rule, then have Gillian do it herself. Gillian nodded in the right places and did as she was told, but with a lack of enthusiasm Susana had never witnessed in a student before. In her experience, kids generally started out starry-eyed over the horses, and then either got disillusioned over the hard work involved or accepted it as part of the deal. Gillian seemed disillusioned from the start.

It was almost heartbreaking how excited

Barrymore was to get saddled. He was so responsive and eager to please.

Susana started Gillian on circles. Gillian's performance wasn't brilliant, but she did appear to be making an effort.

Part of being a good teacher was figuring out how an individual student learned best. Susana tried all the usual things. She used cones to help Gillian visualize the circle. She drew the exercise on paper. She demonstrated it herself on Leda.

By the end of the lesson, Gillian hadn't exactly had a huge breakthrough, but that was all right. They'd made a start, laid a foundation. Time would take care of the rest.

She showed Gillian how to give Barrymore a treat, holding her hand flat to protect it from being bitten. Barrymore's strong teeth daintily skimmed over Gillian's palm to pick up the treat, and Susana caught the ghost of a smile on Gillian's face.

But by the end of the second lesson, she was starting to wonder if Gillian wanted to learn to ride at all. Kevin had said Gillian was wild about horses and eager to take riding lessons, but she was showing as much enthusiasm as if she was getting a root canal. Maybe Kevin was projecting some old unfulfilled childhood desires onto his child. It happened. And now, either he was too blind to see the truth, or he was determined to get his money's worth, so to speak, whether Gillian liked it or not.

As delicately as she could, she asked Gillian if she wanted to learn to ride. She didn't want to imply criticism of Gillian's performance, but if Gillian really didn't want to be there, it was best to get that out in the open and figure out another arrangement with Kevin.

"I do want to," Gillian said, looking Susana straight in the eye for once.

"All right," Susana said. "But if something's bothering you, you can tell me."

"Okay," Gillian mumbled.

Things didn't get better. And early in the third lesson, they finally came to a head.

"Look in the direction you want to go," Susana said as Gillian struggled to take Barrymore around the circle. It was something she said a lot with new students, because it naturally put the body in the right position to tell the horse where to go. A horse could feel a fly on its back, so when a rider looked where she wanted to go, the horse could feel that, too.

"Chin up," she said. She'd been saying that a lot, too.

Then Gillian swiped the back of her hand across her eyes, and Susana realized she was crying.

"Gillian? What's wrong?"

Was she hurt? Sick?

Gillian started sobbing in earnest. Susana took Barrymore's lead rope—she'd left his halter on and put the lead rope around the saddle horn—and led him to the mounting block.

"Give me the reins," she told Gillian. "Now climb down."

Gillian did as she said, still crying. Susana steered her toward a bench and sat her down. Then she secured Barrymore's lead rope to a fence and sat beside Gillian.

She set a hand on the girl's shoulder. "What's wrong?"

"I'm terrible at everything!" Gillian burst out. "You keep telling me what to do and I just can't do it. I don't know why I'm so stupid. You're so nice, and Barrymore is such a good horse, and I want to do things right, but I can't. I can't!"

Her words dissolved in another flood of tears. Susana put her arms around her and let her sob.

When the sobs had subsided to shuddering breaths, Susana pulled Gillian back and looked her in the eye.

"I'm going to ask again, Gillian, and I want you to be straight with me," she said. "Do you want to be here taking horseback riding lessons? Do you even like horses?"

Gillian's eyes widened in amazement. "Are you kidding?" she wailed. "I love horses! I'd do anything to be able to ride like the kids at school. But they all come from farms and ranches, so they grew up doing that stuff. I just have my dad. He tries, but he doesn't know either. He didn't even want me to come live with him in the first place. My mom said he wanted to spend time with me and get to know me, but that's not true. She just wanted me out of the way because her new boyfriend doesn't like kids. Dad didn't have a choice."

The words tumbled out in a rush. Gillian had just spoken more to Susana in the past minute than she'd said in all her other lessons combined. And she wasn't finished yet.

"When he said I was going to have riding lessons, I—I thought this was my big chance. I thought maybe if I was super careful and didn't mess up, I could learn. But I'm no good at it. I'm no good at anything! I'm hopeless."

"Listen to me, Gillian. You are not hopeless. You're just a beginner. Riding a horse is a complex skill. There are a lot of things you have to do at the same time, and no one can do them all perfectly right from the start. In the beginning, you're going to make a lot of mistakes. That's just part of the learning process. But if you stick with it and keep trying, you'll slowly start to get it. Your body will learn to do the things your mind has been telling it to do all along. It just takes time and repetition."

"I don't think my body will ever learn.

I'm no good at any kind of sports or...or anything. I'm just stupid and clumsy."

"No. You're not stupid, and you're not clumsy."

"Then why can't I do anything right?"

"Because you don't believe you can. It sounds like you've had a lot of bad experiences while trying to learn new physical skills, and you built up a mental habit of thinking you couldn't do it. And that kind of habit makes itself come true. But habits can be changed. Out here, it's just you and me and the horses. No one else is watching. You can take all the time you need. And if you pay attention to what I tell you and keep trying, you'll get there."

Gillian sniffed. "You really think so?"

"I know so. You've had to learn other complex skills before, all your life. You didn't always know how to walk, but you do now, and you don't even have to think about it anymore. That's called muscle memory. And with enough time and repetition, muscle memory is going to kick in, and riding a horse is going to feel as natural to you as walking."

Gillian gave Susana a long look. Her

eyes and nose were swollen, her skin was blotchy and she suddenly looked a lot younger.

"Okay," Gillian said at last. "But please don't get mad at me. I'm not trying to ignore you when you tell me eyes up, and chin up, and steady hands, and look at where you want to go, and all that. I want to do it. I really do."

"I know that. And I'm not being impatient with you when I keep repeating those things. That's just part of the job. I know you can't remember, so I'm reminding you, because I'm your teacher."

Gillian let out a long shuddery sigh. "Okay," she said again. "I guess I should get back on."

"Let's not today," said Susana. "Horses can sense your emotions, and right now yours are all mixed up. In fact, that might have been part of the problem you were having. Barrymore could tell that you were upset, and that made him worried."

Gillian's chin trembled. "I'm sorry I worried him. He's such a good horse."

"He is a good horse, and he's kind of lonely. How about if for the rest of your lesson time today, you give him a nice long grooming session? He'd love that. He doesn't get much attention."

"Why not?"

"His owner isn't able to come see him very much. Barrymore gets plenty of food and care, but he's on his own a lot."

A few minutes later, Barrymore was still tied to the fence by his lead rope and Gillian was grooming the heck out of him with the currycomb. Barrymore's eyes were half closed with pleasure. Gillian's tears were dried, and she had a faint dreamy smile on her face.

At the end of her lesson, when her father came to pick her up, Gillian gave Susana a big smile and said, "See you next time!"

Susana was physically and emotionally drained, but also happy. She headed to the house to brew a fresh pot of coffee.

Roque met her on the way.

"I have something to show you," he said.

Susana had seen Roque come back earlier from picking up feed, but hadn't checked in with him for a while. Now he was giving her that boyish grin. There was no telling what he'd been up to.

"Is it another dozer?" she asked.

"Ha ha! No. Come on. It's up by the house."

He led her to the yard—really just a small fenced area off the house with nothing in it but a scraggly Texas sage barely clinging to life. Or at least that's all it had had in it the last time Susana had seen it. Now it was filled with a bunch of plastic tubs and wooden boxes, all of which were filled with dirt.

"What is this?" she asked.

"It's your new garden!" said Roque.

She looked at him. "My what?"

"Your garden! Remember the other day, you were saying how you love fresh greens and tomatoes but don't like going to town for them? I thought, why not grow your own?"

"So you decided to make me a garden?"

"Well, there were a few steps in between. See, I was at the feed store earlier today, and I looked at the bulletin board to see what was going on in town, and I saw a flyer from a lady who was giving away old livestock watering troughs for free. I knew we needed some for Rufus and Theophilus, and figured we might as well stock up if she had more than one. So I went over to take a look. The troughs were no good for holding water. One of them had a puncture in the bottom, and the other had a long tear running down the side. But as I was standing there looking, I realized they'd be perfect to use in a container garden. And when I said that, the lady said she had some old wooden crates I could use, too, made with untreated lumber. Then her neighbor said she had some old cold frames that had belonged to her father, and I might as well take them, too, because she didn't garden anymore. I got the whole lot for free, along with a spade, a rake, a hoe and some of those nifty little seed starters!"

Susana felt her jaw hanging open. She didn't know what to say. But Roque kept on talking.

"I brought them all home, drilled some holes in the bottom for drainage and got them set up. I picked up some Styrofoam packing blocks from Darcy's Hardware, put them in the bottom for drainage and covered them with some landscape cloth. Then I added some nice aged compost from that place in town that sells gravel and mulch and stuff. You know, there's no reason you can't set up a fine composting system out here. The horse manure is a great source of nitrogen. I checked the planting requirements for this zone. It's early February now, which means we'll be able to plant onions, greens, sugar snap peas and broccoli transplants soon. Then in March, we can add some tomatoes, maybe some basil. Won't that be great?"

He folded his arms over his chest. He looked extremely pleased with himself.

It was time for her to speak up.

"Wow! This is so thoughtful. Thank you."

"You look worried," he said.

"Yeah, well, I'm not sure I'll have time to maintain it, on top of everything else I've got going on."

He gave her a heart-melting smile. "But you have me now. And I come from a long line of Portuguese and Italian immigrants who grew amazing vegetables in container gardens set up on apartment balconies. And a container garden is just what you need out here, with this thin stony soil."

He snapped his fingers. "Oh! Before I forget, there's something else I need to tell you. I got another client!"

"For boarding? Lessons?"

"Not exactly. See, the lady who was giving away the watering troughs, and her neighbor who gave me the cold frames and garden tools, they thought the container garden was for me at first, but I told them no, it was for my boss. So they wanted to know where I worked, and I told them about this place. And then the cold frame lady went and got their other neighbor, who has a son who wants to ride."

"How old a son?"

"Oh, midthirties, I guess. He did two tours in Afghanistan."

"Oh! An adult student."

"No, not a student. He already knows how to ride. He just hasn't done it in a long time, ever since his injury."

"What kind of injury?"

"Well, see, the thing is, he's blind."

Susana must have misunderstood him. "Blind? He's blind?"

"Yeah. So he just needs a safe place to ride, is all."

Susana was dumbfounded. This sounded like a liability nightmare.

"He knows the risk," Roque added quickly. "He'll sign a waiver and all that. He doesn't want to do anything fancy, just go on trail rides with other people. So I thought, what better place for that than out here?"

Susana didn't know whether to laugh or cry. "Roque, we don't have any trails!"

"Not yet, but we will. All we have to do is finish the first one, and the guy can get started. We always knew we were going to do it. Now we have a deadline."

"Having a deadline for something doesn't make it get done!"

Roque put his hands on her shoulders and looked down at her as if she were a small child. "We'll get it done."

He was so sure of himself. Susana wished she could share his confidence, and be sure the whole thing wouldn't come crashing down around her.

"I know you like to have all your ducks in a row," he went on. "But sometimes opportunities come along and you have to act on them. You can't always wait for everything to be perfect before you begin. You have to jump right in there and build around you as you go."

Before Susana could point out that the dozer still wasn't running, and they hadn't even finished the chainsaw work on the trail, a beat-up truck pulled into the driveway.

"Oh, good," said Roque. "Curt's here."

"Curt?" said Susana. "Who's Curt?"

"A guy I know from Lalo's. He wants to buy a horse. A rescue. And he wants to buy it from you."

Curt turned out to be a man in his late twenties, dressed in worn, dirty jeans and a T-shirt so faded that Susana couldn't guess its original color. Roque made the quickest of introductions before ducking out. Before he left, he took Susana by the shoulder again, leaned close to her and said, "Don't worry. Curt's a solid guy."

And without another word, he was gone. Now Susana was getting angry. Ordinarily she would vet people before selling a horse to them, but how could she tell that to Curt when he was already here? And what did Roque mean when he said Curt wanted to buy a rescue and wanted to buy it from her? Was he looking for something cheap? Did he have the means to properly care for a horse, or would he stick it in a cramped lot and neglect it?

Well, she could go ahead and take him around to look at the horses today, anyway. If he still wanted to buy after that, she would explain her vetting process—personal references, farrier reference, home visit, the whole nine yards. That might put an end to his interest right there.

And after she dealt with Curt, she was going to have words with Roque.

She took Curt around to all the rehabilitated horses that she was willing to sell. When they reached the strawberry roan mare that Susana called Contessa, he let out a low whistle. "Look at those lines," he said softly. "Perfect conformity. Where'd you find her?"

Well! Curt had an eye for quality, anyway.

"At auction," Susana said. "She was skin and bones."

But even then, she'd known the mare was something out of the ordinary. And after she'd brought her home, she'd found her tattoo and looked up her ID number. It turned out that Contessa, in spite of falling on hard times in recent years, had come from some very distinguished bloodlines.

"How much?" asked Curt.

More than you can afford, my friend.

Susana named her high, but not unfair, price.

"Done," said Curt. He reached into his back pocket and took out his wallet.

"I know you'll need to check my references," he said. "In the meantime, I'd like to give you a fifty percent deposit. Is that acceptable?"

He was already peeling off crisp bills of large denominations.

Susana just stared. What the heck? Was the guy a drug dealer?

He glanced over at her and smiled. "I like to pay small business owners in cash whenever I can. I was a small business owner myself once, not too long ago."

She found her voice at last. "What is it that you do, exactly?"

"I make alternative housing."

"Alternative?"

"Adobe, straw bale. That kind of thing."

He explained how he traveled the country, spearheading building projects for clients. Reading between the lines, Susana understood that these were very select, very rich clients, and that Curt was a very rich man, and a respected expert in a highly specialized field.

And here she'd been making a judgment about him based solely on his dirty clothes!

"Do you live in this area?" she asked.

"I keep a house in Limestone Springs. I like to come here during the winter months. That's where I'll keep Contessa."

"And you know Roque from Lalo's Kitchen?"

"Oh, yes. He talks about you a lot. He's proud of you, you know. You're doing good work here, Susana, rescuing these horses, giving them another shot at life. I'm happy to be able to support that in some small way."

She wouldn't have called it a small way. The wad of cash he'd just handed her was…substantial. Enough to fund a whole lot of fencing, and put a considerable dent in what she'd need for her big barn. And that was only half of the total price!

She wrote him out a receipt for the deposit, and he gave her the contact information for his personal references, farrier and veterinarian. They arranged a home visit later in the week.

Susana was still in shock as Curt drove away. Surely this day couldn't hold any more surprises.

Then Roque came driving up in the dozer.

He was grinning from ear to ear, his chest puffed up with pride. He drove right up to her and stopped.

"Well," he said, swinging himself down to the ground, "I did it! The last part I needed came in today. That's why I had to run off and couldn't stick around with you and Curt. How'd it go with him, anyway?"

Susana let out a choked laugh, then threw her arms around Roque.

"Hey!" he said. He sounded surprised, but not too surprised to hug her back. "What's this for?"

"For being you. You really are the best, Roque. The best partner and the best friend."

"Aw, shucks. You're gonna make me blush."

"I mean it. The way you drum up business and generally go above and beyond expectations… It's fantastic, and it's exactly what I need. Just…try to keep me in the loop a little better from now on, okay?"

"Sure. I can do that. I just get an idea, and then I get a little excited, you know?"

Yes, she knew. And maybe, just maybe, she could find it in herself to trust him a little more.

CHAPTER TWELVE

THEY KNOCKED OUT the last of the chainsaw work in half a day, and celebrated afterward with take-out pizza and beer from Lalo's Kitchen. Stage One was complete. The following day, they started on Stage Two—the dozer work.

This stage was pure fun. Progress was visible and fast. Roque loved driving the dozer, feeling its power, watching all the long thorny branches of mesquite and huisache wave and fall before the metal blade, hearing the rip of cedar stumps torn up by the roots, and looking over his shoulder to see the broad blazed track in his wake. Every so often, when enough accumulated limbs and rocks and cactus fronds built up, he'd push them all out of the way and over to the side of the trail into a brush pile. They'd planned for this ahead of time—at least, Susana had planned and told Roque what to do. She'd figured out exactly where the brush piles should go, and where to put the paths leading to them from the trail, like exit ramps off a highway. It amazed him how her mind worked. She was a natural planner, always looking ahead, spotting potential difficulties and heading them off.

A week or so into February, they had quite a few of those brush piles, all situated in places that would be good for burning later on, once the wood dried out some more and the burn ban lifted. At some point before then, Roque figured he'd come back to the piles with a chainsaw and cut the bigger hardwood pieces into firewood to sell. With the snowstorm so fresh in the town's collective memory, people were pretty keen on stocking up on firewood. Might as well take advantage of that and bring in a little extra income for the business.

Roque pushed a final load of cleared brush, stumps and dirt up the exit ramp and into the current brush pile, then shut off the dozer's ignition. The roaring engine shuddered to a stop. He'd have liked to keep going, but the sun had set a few minutes earlier and it would be dark soon. Susana had already left to take care of evening feeding by herself.

As he stepped down, he heard her call out, "It's beginning to look like an honest-to-goodness riding trail, isn't it?"

She was coming his way with Pirko trotting ahead of her.

"Sure is," said Roque. "I don't have far to go to close the loop. Another full day ought to do it."

Once that was done, they'd have to make a second pass with the dozer, grading the ground and generally tidying up. Then the trail would be ready for Garrett, the blind veteran who wanted to ride. Garrett was eager to start. He'd already been out to visit the facility and get acquainted with the horse he was going to ride—a calm, steady buckskin called Clem.

"Hungry?" Susana asked.

"Starving," said Roque.

"Good. I ordered us some pizza and garlic knots from Lalo's—two pizzas this time, so you can have one all to yourself. It's already paid for. Just has to be picked up."

"Ooh, that sounds good. I think I just drooled a little bit. Thanks for doing that. You don't have to keep feeding me all the time, but I'm glad you do."

"I might as well. I've given up on you ever making an accurate log of your hours, or limiting them to twenty per week. I've got to make up the difference somehow."

Zac's construction business had picked up enough to give Roque thirty hours or so of work a week, making it a challenge to fit in another twenty-plus at Susana's place, but he'd managed it. Zac was willing to be flexible, since Roque was helping Zac's cousin.

It felt good to be busy. Those days of lying around on his mattress in the horse trailer, staring up at the ceiling, were gone like a bad dream. It was hard to believe that only a month and a half ago he'd been bored and lonely and on the brink of giving up.

Roque and Susana walked back toward the house together in the fading sunlight. Pirko led the way, her plumy tail waving high.

Roque went inside the house and washed his hands at the kitchen sink.

"I'll go pick up the pizza," he said.

"Be sure to come straight home with it," Susana replied. "Don't get sidetracked into making any new business deals. I know how you are."

He took the towel from its bar and dried his hands, leaning his hip against the countertop. "Hmm. What if it's a really good deal?"

"No, not even then. I'm tired and hungry. I just want to eat my dinner and go to bed."

"What if it's a *spectacular* deal? Are you really willing to miss out on a spectacular deal just because you're a little tired?"

She considered. "How about a compromise? If you do meet any potential clients or students or customers or investors or whatever, don't bring them here tonight. Just take their numbers and tell them I'll get back to them."

"You've got a deal. Hey, look at that! I already made one and I haven't even left yet."

Lalo's Kitchen was a casual dining and take-out place located in an old refurbished downtown building, right next door to Tito's Bar, with a big pass-through connecting the two businesses.

Jenna, the assistant manager at Lalo's, saw Roque come in. "Hi, Roque. Are you here to pick up Susana's order? It's almost ready. I'll have it out in a few minutes."

Roque took a seat at the bar and looked around. He could put names to about half the faces in this place. The kid sitting at the two-top table with textbooks spread out in front of her was Halley, Jenna's daughter. Any time Jenna was at Lalo's, Halley was there, too. Jenna homeschooled her, and the dad didn't seem to be in the picture. The muscle-bound guy at the end of the bar was Bart, who owned the gym downtown, and next to him was Mad Dog McClain, the fire chief. Mad Dog wasn't all that mad, as far as Roque could see. He was a mild-mannered gardener who wore a lot of sunscreen because of his red hair and fair complexion. Three of the Mendoza brothers had just taken a booth together—Johnny, Enrique and Eddie. Their youngest brother, Tito, owned the bar next door. There was another Mendoza brother out in the oil fields of West Texas, but Roque had never met him. Jimmy Ray from the feed store caught Roque's eye and raised his beer in a greeting. Roque waved back. He liked knowing who all these people were and how they were connected to each other, and being waved at and spoken to in a friendly way and not shunned and glared at all the time. His social life had done a complete one-eighty since Susana had come into it.

A young woman in a ruffled top, with big blue eyes, gold hoop earrings and long brown hair, was watching Roque from a table nearby. She looked familiar, but he couldn't quite place her.

She smiled at him. "I'm Monika Vrba," she said. "Susana's sister. I've seen you before at my parents' shop."

"Oh, yeah! That's where I know you from. You look like Susana—the eyes and the hair. You're taller, though."

She chuckled. "Yeah, but then a lot of people are taller than Susana. I passed her up in height when I was just six years old and she was ten."

Roque wasn't sure he'd heard right. "You were six and she was ten?"

"That's right. You know why she's so tiny, right? It's because she was born early. She was very premature, just thirty-two weeks."

"No. No, I didn't know that."

"Mmm-hmm. It was touch and go for a while, whether she'd make it. But she's always been a fighter."

"Yeah. Always sticking up for the little guy, and looking after anyone who needs extra care."

"Exactly."

Monika held his gaze a second longer, like she was sizing him up, or sending him a wordless message, or both.

Just then, Jenna came back with Susana's order.

Roque picked up the boxes. "Thanks, Jenna. Nice meeting you, Monika."

"Same here," said Monika. "Will we see you tomorrow?"

"What's tomorrow?"

"The Chili Noodle Soup Supper."

"Oh, yeah. Your mom was telling me about that."

"It's a good time. You and Susana should come."

"I'll mention it to her," Roque said, but he could already hear Susana say it was too far away and she couldn't leave the horses.

The smell of hot pizza filled his truck and made his stomach growl all the way home—or all the way back to Susana's place, anyway, which more often than not he thought of as home. The horse trailer on the town lot was just a place to sleep at night.

Susana had the table set with white plates and a red-and-white checked tablecloth, and she'd already set a can of Thirsty Goat, Roque's favorite locally brewed craft beer from Tito's Bar, at his place, along with a pint glass. He'd brought over a six-pack of Thirsty Goat to keep in her fridge, and another of the Lake Breeze Blonde that Susana liked.

Roque's pizza was topped with sausage, bell peppers, black olives and provolone. Susana's had brussels sprouts, red onions, goat cheese and mushrooms. Roque liked it, but not as much as the sausage kind.

"Oh, man, this is fantastic," he said through a mouthful. "I'm so glad we've got good pizza in Limestone Springs, even if we do have to drive to town to get it."

"Yeah, the nearest chain pizza place is too far away to deliver out here," said Susana. "But they don't have anything as good as *this*."

"We had some great pizza places in Jersey City," said Roque. "Carmine's, Georgio's, Renato's, Gino's. I ought to take you there one day. Show you the old stomping ground."

He kept his tone light, but just for a second he imagined doing it. Taking her to meet his parents, his brothers and sisters. Introducing her as—what? His boss? His friend? His girlfriend?

Susana chuckled. "I don't know, Roque. Jersey City's kind of far away. I don't see how I could go there and be back in time to feed horses."

"Oh, hey, that reminds me. I saw your sister Monika at Lalo's. She asked if we were going to the Chili Noodle Soup Supper tomorrow."

Susana didn't ask what connection an

imaginary pizza-eating trip to Jersey City could possibly have to a church-sponsored supper in a rural Texas town. She just said, "I didn't know you knew Monika."

"I don't, or I didn't. She introduced herself. She recognized me from the shop."

"Hmm, yeah, I guess she would. You're kind of a local celebrity."

He waited. "So?"

"So what?"

"So do you want to go?"

"To the supper? I'd like to, but it's a long drive, and we'd have to be back in time to feed horses."

"It wouldn't be that hard. An hour to get there, two hours to eat and hang out, and an hour back. It's doable."

He kept his eyes on his food, but he could feel her watching him.

"Do you want to go?" she asked.

"Me? Sure. Chili and noodles and ko-laches, what's not to love? Plus it would be part of my Texas education, seeing an authentic Czexan community."

He was also just plain curious. He wanted to see this place where Susana's family had come from and where she'd spent so much time as a kid.

"It's okay if you don't want me to go," he said. "I guess it might be a little weird because of, you know."

"Because of what?"

"You know. That day at the shop when we saw your mom, and she thought there was something going on between the two of us, and you...let her think that."

He stole a quick glance at Susana. She had her eyes fixed on him, but he couldn't read her expression.

"Yeah, well," she said at last, "it was easier than trying to set her straight."

"No, I get that," Roque said quickly. "It's just—well, maybe you're thinking it would be hard to keep it up at the supper. More time, more relatives, more questions."

"I guess it would. But it doesn't matter because I can't be away from the horses for that long anyway."

Roque picked up two more slices of pizza. "You know, at some point, you're going to get to where you can afford an evening off once in a while if you want, or even a whole weekend. This place is really going to take off, and you'll be able to hire more help."

She sighed. "Sometimes I think that's never going to happen."

"Sure it will. We're going to finish that first trail, and add more trails, and charge people to ride them. Then you're going to be able to build that big nice barn so you can take on more boarders."

"I wish it were that simple."

"Isn't it?"

"Not really. A big raised center aisle barn like I want is expensive. Even with all the trails up and running, it'll be a long time before I have the funds to build it."

"Well then, maybe you need more high-paying clients to balance out all your low-paying ones and your hard-luck cases."

"I don't have anything to offer people like that."

"Sure you do. You just have to figure out what they want and how to give it to them. What you can offer that other places can't."

She smiled at him. "Maybe I should leave that to you. You have a gift for spinning deals out of thin air. I don't know how you do it."

He shrugged. "It's not that big a thing. I just see the connections that need to be made, and make them."

"It is a big thing. When you make those connections, and bring the right people together, the situation takes on a life of its own. You're like a master facilitator."

"Well, you're the heart and soul of this place. If it wasn't for you, there'd be nothing for me to facilitate."

They talked about horses and barns and tossed pizza crusts to Pirko until Susana's phone alarm went off.

"Is it time for night check already?" asked Roque. "I better hit the road."

He carried their dishes to the dishwasher while Susana bagged up what was left of the pizza.

"You want to do night check with me?" she asked.

"Sure."

They walked silently down the lane together, checking the animals in their pens along each side. The horses stood relaxed and quiet, tails swishing gently, one hip canted. The donkeys, llama and goat in the last enclosure had recently been joined by a Shetland pony and a Kunekune pig. They all seemed to be getting along fine together.

Roque had gotten to know the place pretty well over the past month and a half—the lay of the land, the placement of the fencing, which animals went where and what food they all got. Cisco was sharing a pen with a grullo gelding named Gunmetal. He came over to say hello, nickering softly and nuzzling Roque's shoulder.

Daisy was starting to show. It probably wouldn't be that much longer before she dropped that foal.

All the horses were settled in for the night—except for one. Meriadoc, the elderly Arabian, was standing in an odd, strained posture, with his head at a weird angle, looking very sorry for himself.

Roque felt Susana tensing beside him. She slid between the bars of the gate, walked over to Meriadoc and laid her ear against his side.

"What are you listening for?" asked Roque.

"Gut sounds," she said.

"Did you hear any?"

She straightened and laid a small gentle hand on Meriadoc's neck. "No."

"So…what does that mean?"

"It means he has colic."

Meriadoc curled his lip and shook his head, like he was trying to get rid of flies. He pawed at his belly with a back hoof, then got down on the ground and rolled.

"Help me get him up," said Susana. "Bring me that bridle and lead rope from the gatepost."

They managed to get the bridle on Meriadoc and haul him to his feet with the lead rope, with Roque handling the hauling part. It wasn't easy. Roque was a fairly big guy, and Meriadoc was a small horse, but even a small horse was a lot bigger than a big man.

"Keep him moving," Susana said. "Walk him around his pen—not too fast, just a steady walk. Don't let him lie down. I'm going to call the vet."

Roque started a slow lap around the pen

with Meriadoc. The horse was breathing fast and his coat shone with sweat. Pirko went with them, trotting along at Meriadoc's other side. Roque heard Susana's voice as she talked to the vet but couldn't make out the words.

By the time he was heading back toward the front of the pen, she was off the phone and holding what looked like a small caulk gun.

"The vet's dealing with another case," she said. "He'll be here as soon as he can to see if we need to do surgery."

"Surgery! Whoa! That escalated fast. An hour ago he was fine, and now he needs surgery?"

Susana sighed. "I hope not. Surgery would be risky at Meriadoc's age, besides being wildly expensive. The condition could sort itself out before the vet even gets here. I hope it does. In the meantime, we give him Banamine and keep walking him."

Roque was still heading her way with Meriadoc. Susana took the cap off the end of the syringe and spun a ring around at the opposite end until she had it where she wanted it.

"What is that stuff?" Roque asked. "What'll it do for him?"

"It's a nonsteroidal anti-inflammatory and painkiller. It's like ibuprofen for horses. It won't cure whatever's wrong with him, but it'll make him more comfortable, which will make him less likely to hurt himself, or us."

She came to Meriadoc's right side, where Roque was, and took hold of the halter. The second Roque stopped walking, Meriadoc tried to lie down.

"Keep him up!" Susana said.

Roque planted his feet on the ground, braced himself and held on with all his might. He saw Susana stick her finger in the corner of the horse's mouth and insert the syringe. Meriadoc started to make chewing motions. Susana pushed the syringe's plunger.

"Keep his head up," she said. "We don't want any of it to fall out of his mouth."

Meriadoc went on working his lips and tongue. Roque could see his throat ripple as he swallowed the stuff down.

"Okay, let's get him moving again," said Susana.

They started walking.

"What exactly is colic, anyway?" Roque asked. "I've heard of it, and I know it's bad, but I've never actually been around a horse that had it before. What causes it?"

"A lot of things can cause it. Colic is a symptom, not a disease. It just means abdominal pain. Intestinal displacement, impaction, torsion, strangulation—any of those could lead to colic. Or there could be a dietary cause, like if a horse that had never had alfalfa suddenly ate a lot of it."

"That couldn't have happened with Meriadoc, though. He always has the exact same diet every day."

"Yeah, well, sometimes they just get it and you don't know why. Meriadoc's always had a sensitive GI tract, and it's getting worse as he gets older."

She patted the horse's neck. "I know you don't feel good, buddy. We're going to take care of you. Right now we just need you to keep walking."

"What's the point of all the walking?"

"It gives him something to do other

than think about how bad he feels, and keeps him from lying down and kicking at his belly and getting all twisted up inside. Colic can turn bad quickly and kill the horse, so you want to take every precaution possible."

"For how long?"

"As long as it takes," Susana said grimly.

Roque noticed that she hadn't actually asked him to stay. Maybe she was afraid he'd say no. Or maybe she knew she didn't have to ask, because there was no way he was going to drive off and leave her to deal with a sick horse all by herself.

"You don't have to keep walking," he said. "It only takes one of us to lead him around, and it should be me in case he tries to go down again."

She hesitated. "I don't want to put it all on you."

"I can take it. You should save your strength. I've got this."

"Well… I guess I could go make us some coffee. We might be awake awhile."

"Good thinking. It'll keep us warm, too."

She started to go, then turned back and said, "Thanks, Roque."

She was back within ten minutes, bringing two commuter mugs. She set Roque's on top of the cedar fence post where the halter had hung. Every once in a while, when passing that way, he'd grab it and take a few swallows.

She tried again to take over walking Meriadoc.

"Susana, let me do this," Roque said. "I'm bigger and stronger, and it makes sense for me to do it. There's no reason for you to wear yourself out when I'm here."

Pirko stayed right with him the entire time. She quickly figured out that Susana and Roque wanted Meriadoc to stay on his feet, so whenever the horse tried to get down and roll, she'd nip at his hocks. It helped.

An hour passed, then two hours. The moon rose and the stars came out. Every so often, Meriadoc would try to lie down, and Roque fought to keep him up. It was quite a workout.

The vet called back. Susana listened,

then said, "All right. We'll see you when you get here."

She hung up.

"Is he on his way?" Roque asked.

"No. He says he's still at least an hour out. He was in Schraeder Lake taking care of a goat that was having a difficult birth, and by the time he got that sorted out, another one of the goats had gone into labor, and she had a hard time, too."

About halfway through the third hour, Roque said, "It's been a while since he tried to roll. Do you think he's getting better?"

"Maybe. Or it might just mean the Banamine kicked in, which makes him feel better in the short run. Stop him for a bit and I'll have another listen."

She laid her ear against Meriadoc's side again, listened awhile and shook her head.

"Still no gut noises. Here, give me the lead rope. Now that he's stopped trying to lie down, I'll take a turn walking him while you rest."

Roque hadn't realized how tired he was until he stopped moving. His feet were sore, and his back, arms and legs ached from all the wrestling he'd been doing with the horse. He stretched, arching his back and rolling his neck, then rolled his left arm. Once he'd gotten most of the kinks worked out, he finished the last of his coffee, then went inside to get them some water bottles.

Back in the pen, he stood awhile staring at Meriadoc's big haunches and hard hooves that could crush an unprotected human foot.

"It's funny what delicate animals horses are," he said. "They're so big and powerful, but they can be hurt so easily."

"That's because they've been bred for qualities other than hardiness. It's different with wild horses. Mustangs are hardy because only the strong survive long enough to breed. The weak don't stand a chance. Meriadoc never would have made it to adulthood in the wild, with his sensitive stomach and his weak hooves."

She patted the horse's neck. "I wish I could make him better. I hate it when an animal is suffering."

"You're doing all you can for him."

"I know. I just wish I could be sure that

it'll be enough." Her chin trembled and she blinked rapidly. "If he were some prize horse belonging to a client, or any client's horse, you can bet I'd be doing everything I could to save him. Meriadoc's little and old, but he can't help that. He deserves to be taken care of just as much as if he had a fancy pedigree."

Something inside Roque's chest swelled up, and his throat got all tight. She was so small and so fierce. She was the most kindhearted and generous person he knew, and the strongest.

Please, God, let Meriadoc pull through.

At the end of an hour, he took over walking Meriadoc again. The old horse looked tired. His steps were labored and his face was more drawn than usual. But he kept putting one foot in front of the other.

Pirko was tired, too. By now she was taking occasional breaks, but after a few minutes she always got up again and went back to lapping the pen with Meriadoc and whichever one of them was walking him.

"You want to go inside and get some rest?" Roque asked. "I can keep walking him, and let you know if the vet shows or if he takes a turn for the worse."

"I wouldn't be able to sleep, not knowing what was going on out here," said Susana.

"Then set up a bedroll or something out here. At least that way you can lie down for a while and shut your eyes."

She thought a moment. "I do have a camp mattress I could set up."

She went back to the house and came back with a rolled-up foam mattress and some blankets.

"This sure would be a good time for that big barn you want, wouldn't it?" Roque asked. "You could keep a real mattress out there on an actual bedframe, with maybe a coffee maker and a little fridge. It'd make these nighttime vigils a lot easier."

"Oh, believe me, it's occurred to me," Susana said as she spread the blankets over the mattress.

With a sigh, she lay down and pulled the covers over her. "I'll just shut my eyes for a few minutes. Then I'll take another turn."

"Go ahead. Take as long as you need to."

By the time he finished his next lap, he could see that she was asleep. Lying there curled up on her side, she looked impossibly small and fragile, but Roque knew how tough she was.

The night wore on, and he kept walking.

CHAPTER THIRTEEN

Susana woke in a panic, knowing instinctively that she'd been asleep a lot longer than a few minutes. Something soft was curled up behind her knees. A cat—Haystack. He hurried off in a huff when she sat up.

It was still dark, but the moon had moved to the other side of the sky.

And there was Meriadoc, walking toward her along the fence, with Roque holding his lead rope. All was well, or well enough, at least for now.

She checked the time on her phone. Three a.m. It had been just after midnight when she'd shut her eyes.

"You should have woken me," she called out.

Roque laughed. "Yeah, like I would do that. You needed the sleep."

She ran to catch up to him, fell into step

beside him and reached for the lead rope. "Well, so do you. Here, I'll take over now. You go rest."

He handed over the lead rope. "If it looks like he's going to try to lie down again, you tell me, you hear?"

"I will. Has he tried it lately?"

"Not for a while now. I tried listening for those gut noises. I don't know what they're supposed to sound like, but I didn't hear anything."

"If you heard them, you would know," said Susana.

Just then, Meriadoc stopped in his tracks. Susana tugged the lead rope, but he wouldn't budge. He didn't try to lie down, either, just stood there with a funny look on his face.

Then he let out a load of manure.

"Well, look at that!" said Roque. "That's got to be good, right?"

"It's certainly a step in the right direction," said Susana. "His face doesn't look as strained anymore."

Meriadoc blew air out of his cheeks and gave his head a light toss.

Just then, Susana heard the sound of an

approaching engine. "Aaaaand there's the vet, right on cue," she said.

The vet looked rumpled and exhausted. "Sorry to be so late," he said as he came into the pen. "The goat farm ended up with two sets of quadruplets."

"Whoa!" said Roque. "What are the odds of that?"

"Too great for me to calculate right now," said the vet. "Then one of the does had a prolapse, so I had to wash everything off and put it all back where it belonged and fix it to where it wouldn't fall out again. I guess this is Meriadoc? How's he doing? Any change?" He saw the manure. "Bowel activity?"

"Yes, just now," said Susana.

"Good. Let's have a listen."

The vet took out his stethoscope and put the earpieces in his ears. He laid a hand on Meriadoc's left shoulder and put the stethoscope head at the end of the rib cage, high and low, for about half a minute each, then did the same thing on the right side.

"Gurgling away," he said.

Then Meriadoc reached his head down to the ground, took a bite of dried grass and started to chew as if he didn't have a care in the world.

Susana's heart gave a little leap of joy. Roque smiled at her over the horse's back, looking as relieved as she felt.

There wasn't much left for the vet to do other than check Meriadoc's vitals and say that he appeared to be on the mend. "You can ease up on the walking as long as he seems comfortable and doesn't start rolling again," he said. "Make sure he has a chance to drink plenty of water, and give him some hay. No cubed alfalfa for two days, just hay."

He left not long after that. Now that the crisis was past, Susana felt physically and emotionally drained.

"I guess you can go home now if you want," Susana told Roque. "I mean, of course you can. You could have before. It's not like you need my permission. But, well, if you want to go home—"

"What are you going to do?" Roque asked.

"Stay out here with him awhile longer."

"Then so am I."

"Roque, you've already gone way over on your twenty hours this week."

"I don't care about that. I'm not leaving you alone to deal with this."

She didn't try to argue anymore. In truth, she didn't want him to go.

"Well, go lie down on the mattress, at least," she said.

He started to go, but Susana laid a hand on his arm. "Thank you, Roque. Thank you for staying. I honestly don't think I could have managed last night without you."

His strength and size had been essential in getting and keeping Meriadoc on his feet, and his cheerful attitude had kept her own spirits up. He'd taken as much as he could on himself to spare her, but without making a big show of it.

He smiled down at her, his dark eyes crinkling at the corners, then put a hand over her hand and gave it a squeeze, like he had that time when they'd ridden the four-wheeler together and she'd put her arms around him.

"I'm glad I could help," he said.

He kept his hand on hers. It was warm

and strong. Beneath her palm, she could feel the muscles of his forearm, muscles that had stood out big and taut when he'd wrested Meriadoc around. The hard line of his jaw stood out through the rough black beard. She was suddenly fascinated by the shape of his lower lip. It really was the last word in lower lips. She wanted to touch it with her thumb, her mouth.

He leaned down toward her a fraction of an inch—

Meriadoc let out a loud whuffle.

They instantly turned loose of each other.

"All right then," said Roque. "I'll go take that nap. Wake me if you need me."

She watched him walk over to the mattress and lay his long, lean body down on it. She did need him, and not just for taking care of colicky horses, or blazing trails with the dozer, or creating new business opportunities out of thin air. With his help, and his vision, she was starting to think the equine center could not only survive, but thrive. But beyond that, she needed Roque himself—his irrepressible grin, his endless storehouse of country music lyrics, his presence. He'd been in her life less than two months and she didn't know how she'd ever managed without him.

MERIADOC DIDN'T SHOW any more signs of trouble the rest of the night. He ate a little hay, and drank a lot of water, and dozed. He was probably worn out. Susana was worn out, too, and sore, but that didn't seem to matter anymore. Her aches and fatigue were just part of a beautiful night, along with the moon, and the wind in the trees, and the sharp sparkle of the stars, and the man asleep in the corner of the horse pen.

Around sunrise, she crept over to the mattress to watch Roque sleep. It felt strangely intimate to see him so defenseless.

He opened his eyes, blinked slowly and stretched.

"Hey," he said, his voice rough and groggy. "What's up? Meriadoc okay?"

"He's fine. I'm just going to keep an eye on him a little longer."

Roque was already on his feet. "Let me

do that," he said. "You go inside and get some sleep."

She started to protest, but he cut her off. "No arguing. You're worn out. You can barely put one foot in front of the other. Go on. I'll be here when you wake up."

He took her by the shoulders, spun her around and gave her a push toward the house.

She was too exhausted to do anything but go.

Somehow she managed to reach her front door. Her eyes felt gritty and hot. She stumbled into her bedroom, pulled off her boots, jeans and button-down, and crawled into bed.

She went right to sleep and woke a couple of hours later, feeling wonderfully refreshed. She lay there a few minutes, reveling in happiness, before putting on last night's clothes and going back outside for morning feeding.

But someone had already taken care of it. She could see the horses munching away at their troughs and hear two sets of voices—Roque's and someone else's. There was some activity going on down at the feed barn. Someone was stacking empty feed buckets upside down.

"Gillian?" Susana said. "What are you doing—" Then she remembered. "Oh, we rescheduled your lesson for this morning! I'm so sorry. I completely forgot."

"That's all right," said Gillian. "I got to help Roque with morning feeding, so it worked out fine. He told me about Meriadoc. I'm glad he's better."

"Is he, still?" Susana asked Roque.

"Oh, yeah. He's munching hay and strutting around, looking like he never felt bad a day in his life."

"Good." She turned back to Gillian. "Do you have time to do your lesson now?"

"No, I have to go to San Antonio with my dad. He'll be here any minute."

"Okay. We'll just have to reschedule again."

"Speaking of lessons," said Roque, "I have an idea."

Susana smiled at him. "Of course you do. Let's hear it."

"Well, this morning got me thinking. Gillian's three months of lessons will be up in April or so. Not long after that, school will let out. What if we figured out a little work-study program? Feeding horses, and doing other work around the place, in exchange for lessons?"

Gillian's face lit up. "I would love that! I could come twice a day in the summer, and once a day after school starts up again. Please say yes, Susana."

"I don't know, Gillian," said Susana. "I'll have to think about this. Feeding the horses is a big deal, and it has to be done right. Some of the boarders here have very specific dietary requirements, and if they don't get exactly what they need to eat, they'll get sick."

"But you've got that big chart up in the feed barn that explains the whole thing," said Gillian. "And some of the buckets are different colors, so you can use those for the special diets to help keep track."

"You looked at that chart, huh?"

"Oh, yeah. It made perfect sense. I'm a visual learner."

Susana smiled. "You'd have to get here and have someone drive the feed truck for you."

"My dad can do that, or my grandfather, when my dad's at work. Please, Susana?"

Susana was running out of excuses, and with both Gillian and Roque giving her that wide-eyed, hopeful look, her resistance was fading fast.

"If your dad is okay with this, and we can all come to a mutually beneficial arrangement, then I don't see why we can't trade lessons for labor."

Gillian threw her arms around Susana and squealed. Susana had never seen her so excited.

"Thank you! Thank you! I'm so glad I won't have to give up riding lessons when my three months are up. I'm going to work really hard, and take good care of the horses, and learn to ride really well. Oh, look! There's my dad now! We can get it all settled!"

She ran to meet his truck, leaving Roque and Susana alone.

"Boy, she sure has perked up since she started taking riding lessons," said Roque.

"I know. She used to be so quiet and tense and afraid of her own shadow. I love seeing her so confident. Horseback riding will do that for you."

"Yeah. Especially when you have such a good teacher."

Susana felt light and buoyant as a feather on a breeze. The whole day stretched before her, fresh and full of promise.

"Do you have to work for Zac today?" she asked.

"No. Why?"

"Because I feel like celebrating."

"I'm down with that. What do you have in mind?"

He was so handsome and appealing, with those black curls and those dark dancing eyes with the laugh lines around them. The two of them had pushed through fatigue together, and kept each other going, hour after hour, and now it was morning, and they'd made it. She felt closer to him than ever—close enough to take a chance.

"How would you like to go to Novak for the community-wide Chili Noodle Soup Supper?" she asked.

Roque grinned and pumped his fist in the air.

CHAPTER FOURTEEN

ROQUE FELT FANTASTIC. It was one of those mild, perfect February days in Texas that made up for the bone-chilling north winds, the brutal summer heat and the long stretches of drought. The sky was bright blue, like a piece of jewelry. It was T-shirt-wearing weather—and Roque had on a brand-new T-shirt from the feed store, emblazoned across the chest with the store's logo, taken from the cattle brand that had belonged to Jimmy Ray's great-granddaddy.

Susana stared at the logo. Either that, or she was checking Roque out.

He looked down at himself.

"Is this okay?" he asked. "It isn't a tractor logo. Is it too controversial? Am I underdressed?"

Susana chuckled and brought her gaze back to his eyes. "No. I just didn't real-

ize that the feed store had its own line of
branded T-shirts, and I've got to say I'm a
little surprised Jimmy Ray sprang for the
athletic cut."

Ah, so she'd noticed that.

"Yeah, I talked him into it," said Roque.
"I told him the only way I was going to
wear one was if it was athletic cut."

"I see. I didn't realize you had so much
influence with Jimmy Ray."

"Oh, yeah, me and Jimmy Ray are tight.
I told him that your basic well-built young
cowboy doesn't want a lot of extra fabric
bunching up around his middle. He wants
to show off his sculpted physique."

She nodded. "It was a good call," she
said. "You look nice."

"So do you."

She had on a long-sleeved V-neck T-
shirt in a rich shade of red that really set
off her coloring. Instead of her usual boot-
cut jeans, she wore skinny jeans, tucked
into a pair of cowboy boots he'd never
seen before, embroidered with little ivory
flowers and vines and things.

"Hey!" said Roque. "You're wearing

fancy boots. You didn't tell me this was a fancy boots occasion."

"Stick around Texas long enough and you'll have boots for every occasion," said Susana. "Nice black ones for weddings and funerals, a waterproof pair, some steel toes. They even make a kind lined with Thinsulate for when the weather gets really cold."

"I intend to," said Roque. "Stick around, I mean."

She smiled. "Good."

Roque felt nervous all of a sudden. To cover it up, he knelt down and petted Pirko. She licked him in the face.

He stood up again. "Are you ready to go?"

"I'm ready," said Susana.

She put Pirko inside, locked the front door and followed Roque to his truck. He opened the passenger door for her as usual. The step was a bit high for her, so he gave her his hand to help her up.

They drove east, away from the Hill Country, in the direction of the coast. The land flattened out, and the trees changed. There were fewer cedars, more live oaks, and a lot of palm trees, but all the palms looked dead on top from the snowstorm. Roque asked if they'd come back, and Susana said she didn't know. Once in a while, they passed an oil well with a bright orange flame burning at the top. Before long, Czech-sounding names like Vsetin and Cusack started popping up on street signs and small businesses—meat markets, dance halls, nurseries, bakeries, restaurants.

"It really is a whole other world out here," Susana said.

"Yeah, it looks like it. Why did so many Czechs come to Texas, anyway?"

"Partly because of the availability of land, and partly because of bad conditions in Europe. There were waves of Czech immigration to Texas at different times. My ancestors came early, between the mid-nineteenth century and the First World War, mostly from Moravia and Bohemia. They were farmers back in Europe, and they farmed here, too. Started out as sharecroppers but eventually earned enough to buy their own land. Czech immigrants settled entire areas, and formed these little pockets of Czech culture that are still largely intact."

"Do they still speak the language?"

"Some do. Until about twenty years ago, the church service in Novak was conducted partly in Czech. A lot of the older people are still fluent in it. My parents know it, but they understand it better than they speak it. My brothers and sisters and I know enough to get by—except my brother Mark. He moved to the Czech Republic a few years ago to study the language and history."

She pointed to a big wooden building. "Look, there's a Czech dance hall. There are a lot of them in this area. I used to go every weekend when I was in high school, with Mark and Monika and our cousins."

The dance halls and butcher shops soon gave way to farmland, and the roadway narrowed and turned to gravel. The land was so flat, you could see for miles around.

The church building was situated right next to a neighboring farm, only about a hundred feet off from the white clapboard farmhouse. It was small and old-fashioned, sided in cream-colored limestone, with vaulted ceilings and a steeple. A fenced-off burial ground stood to one side, behind a gravel parking lot.

Roque parked between a truck and an SUV. There seemed to be a lot of trucks and SUVs out here.

He walked around to the passenger door, opened it and gave Susana his hand again to help her down. He felt gigantic beside her. Maybe it was his imagination, but as they started walking, he felt a whole lot of eyes being suddenly drawn to him. Was it because he was a newcomer? Probably not. Susana had said the event was open to the community, and there were a lot of people here. It had to be because he was with her. They were curious about Susana's date—if that's what he was.

A crowd converged on the two of them before they'd made it out of the parking lot. He recognized Monika and Susana's mother, Kristyna, but the rest were strangers. Introductions started, the names flying by too fast for him to possibly keep track—half a dozen siblings, two sets of grandparents, a trio of aunts and several cousins, including Zac, his boss at his construction job. He found his hand being shaken by Susana's father, a big heavy-browed man in a plaid shirt who, unlike her mother, did not invite Roque to call him by his first name.

Kristyna hugged Susana, then hugged Roque, too.

"Roque, I hope you brought an appetite," said Kristyna.

"Oh, yes, ma'am," said Roque. "I came ready for a three-meat meal."

Kristyna laughed and hugged him again.

So much food! Huge kettles of chili and chicken noodle soup, plates of homemade bread and chicken salad sandwiches, sausages and kolaches. Roque filled his plate, glad that he'd brought a hundred-dollar bill for the freewill offering.

He and Susana took a seat at one of the tables that stood outside. Some of Susana's relatives joined them—at least, Roque was pretty sure most of them were relatives. There seemed to be a strong family resemblance in the high cheekbones and blue eyes. They talked about cattle and crops, the high price of feed, how every-one had fared in the snowstorm and how they sure could use some rain.

"How's your horse business, Zuzanka?" asked a gray-haired uncle.

"Business is good," she said. "I even have a hired man now."

The uncle looked Roque over. "Yeah, so I hear. What about that little Arabian you got when the Volciks' farm broke up? Do you still have him?"

"I sure do. As a matter of fact, he just went through a bad bout of colic."

She told them all about Meriadoc's rough night. That got their attention. They listened closely and rejoiced with her on hearing how he'd pulled through. Then they all took turns telling stories about their own rough nights with colicky horses, calving cows, sick bulls or other ailing livestock. The stories got more and more harrowing. Meanwhile, Susana got drawn into a conversation with a younger set sitting on the other side of her. *They* seemed to be talking about fun times they used to have at dance halls when they were teenagers. Roque couldn't hear much of it, because his side of the table was still going on about scours and abscesses and such.

Then Roque heard Susana say his own name.

He couldn't make out everything she was saying, but she seemed to be telling them about the chainsaw he'd fixed, the dozer he'd traded for, the new clients he'd brought in and the nearly finished trail that would be open for trail rides soon. Her father seemed to be picking up on the conversation as well, although, like Roque, he was officially a part of the discussion of veterinary crises. He became a lot friendlier to Roque after that.

Roque finished his first plate of food and went back for seconds and thirds. By then, there'd been some turnover in the people sitting at his end of the table, with Susana's mother and aunts replacing the men, and talk had turned to Bohemian glassware, which he thought was a definite change for the better.

"Our family has so many beautiful pieces, brought over from the Crystal Valley where all the old glassworks used to be," said Kristyna. "Most of them are in the safe-deposit box at the bank, which is a shame. They ought to be worn and enjoyed, not hidden away for safekeeping. Someday I need to sit you girls down and go through it all, and figure out who wants what, and divide it up fairly." She smiled at Roque. "There are a lot of rings in our collection that would make lovely engagement rings. They weren't originally made for that, because engagement rings weren't part of Czech culture back then, but there's no reason they couldn't be used that way today."

"Well, sure!" said Roque.

Susana caught his eye and mouthed the word *sorry*. He smiled at her. He didn't mind. He liked her mother, and it made him happy that she apparently considered him to be suitable son-in-law material.

While he was filling a dessert plate with kolaches, he heard a roar of laughter coming from the table he'd just left. Susana was laughing hard, with her head thrown back and her eyes shut, and she looked so pretty that for a while Roque just stood there, staring.

"Having a good time?"

Monika was standing across the dessert table, getting coffee.

"I am," he said. "I'm glad we came."

She smiled. "I'm glad, too. Glad you managed to drag Susana away from those horses of hers long enough to bring her here."

He chuckled. "It wasn't easy."

She stirred creamer into her coffee. "You know, Valentine's Day is coming up. That would be a good time to make a move—if you wanted to make one."

Roque's heart gave a heavy thump. "Why? Did she say something to you?"

"She didn't have to. I can see how she looks at you. She likes you."

He looked back at Susana. "You really think so?"

"I wouldn't say it if I didn't."

Susana glanced his way, tucking her hair behind her ear in a carelessly graceful gesture. Without taking his eyes off her, Roque said, "Maybe I should make a move. But I want to do it right, make it special. We're together all the time, working. And I love that. But I'd like to get her away from work for a while. She's always taking care of everyone else, people and animals. I'd like to take care of her for a change."

This was the first time he'd voiced his intentions out loud. It made him feel sort of shaky.

"Then you'll have to plan it all out in advance," said Monika. "Figure out every objection she could possibly raise, and take care of it all ahead of time so she can relax."

"The biggest thing would be evening feeding for the horses." He thought of Gillian. "But I might have a work-around for that."

"Good! Where will you go?"

It couldn't be anyplace too fancy. He couldn't afford fancy. But Susana didn't have expensive tastes.

"Maybe I could take her to one of those Czech dance halls that I keep hearing about," he said. "Sort of a dinner and dancing thing."

"Dinner and dancing is good. Just give her notice early enough in the day so she can get ready. She'll want to look her best. She doesn't often get a chance to do her hair and face and put on a cute outfit. Let her make the most of it."

Roque thought some more, then shook his head. "I don't know about this whole surprise thing. Maybe I'm taking too much for granted. I don't know that she'd even want to go out with me on a real date."

"I like your chances. It's not often that she brings a man to meet the family, and when I say not often, I mean it's never happened before."

"Really?" Roque made his decision. "Okay, I'm going to do it. Will you help me? Tell me which dance hall and where to eat and all that?"

"Sure."

He was glad Monika thought he had a shot, but nervous, too. He hoped he wasn't about to mess everything up.

WHILE SUSANA LAUGHED and joked with her siblings and cousins, she kept a wary eye on Roque and Monika. What were they talking about, over there by the kolache table? Whatever it was, it looked pretty serious, and serious was not Roque's usual mode. Susana pretended not to pay attention, but she didn't miss a thing. She saw the glances Roque kept darting her way, thoughtful and uneasy.

He'd seemed uneasy last night, too, when he'd told her about running into Monika at Lalo's while picking up the pizza—almost as if he was testing the waters with Susana, trying to make sure she still wanted the two of them to be friends and coworkers only. Why? Had he suspected that her feelings for him already went well beyond friendship, and was he trying to safeguard against hurting her? Was it possible that the whole reason he'd wanted to come to the Chili Noodle Soup Supper in the first place was to see Monika again?

Well, and why wouldn't he? Monika was pretty and lively and fun-loving. She'd always drawn plenty of male attention wherever she went. If Roque liked her, it was a sign of good taste. And it wasn't as if Susana had any claim on him. He was her hired man, not her boyfriend.

So why did the sight of her hired man and her sister together give her such a horrible hollow feeling inside?

CHAPTER FIFTEEN

THERE WERE FOUR days between the Chili Noodle Soup Supper and Valentine's Day, and Roque needed every minute of that time to plan, and to put his plans into effect. He'd never in his life put this much thought or effort into a date, and he couldn't have managed it now without Monika's help. She'd texted him the info on the Czech dance hall, how to get there and when to leave in order to reach it on time. She'd told him how much time to allow before that, not just for Susana to get ready for the evening, but also to know they were going out to eat so she wouldn't fill up on a big lunch or an afternoon snack. Roque had never known that getting ready for a date could be so complicated. For him, a shower, a clean shirt and a last-minute inspiration had always been enough.

Sorting out the horse feeding was the biggest challenge. He had to get Gillian thoroughly trained ahead of time, to the point where Susana would be confident that Gillian could manage on her own and not spend the whole evening worrying. But he also had to be casual enough about it not to rouse Susana's suspicions. He had to make sure that Gillian was available on the night in question, but if he told her why, he ran the risk that she'd spill the secret to Susana.

It was a risk he had to take. Gillian was excited about the big surprise Valentine's Day date, and proud to be in on the secret. She swore she wouldn't tell, but she might let something slip out without meaning to. Roque was having a hard enough time keeping the secret himself. At one point, while reading a text from Monika, he'd been almost positive that Susana had seen his phone screen. She hadn't said anything, but it had been a near thing.

He had to strike the right balance with the whole evening. He wanted to whisk her away, dazzle her, sweep her off her feet. But he couldn't overpower her with how he had this whole elaborate evening planned and there was nothing she could do about it. He had to give her a chance to say no. When it came right down to it, he didn't even know if she liked him that way. Sometimes he was almost positive that she did, and Monika seemed to think she did, but who knew, really?

He hoped the whole thing wouldn't blow up in his face.

"THERE'S SOMETHING I want to ask you," Roque said.

Susana's heart gave a sickening lurch. Here it came.

Ever since the Chili Noodle Soup Supper, she'd been riding an emotional roller coaster. It didn't help that she'd been seeing so much Valentine's Day merchandise everywhere. H-E-B had a huge display of bouquets, candy, stuffed animals and mini rosebushes at the front of the store. Even the meat aisle had something called a sweetheart steak—a butterflied, boneless, heart-shaped rib eye, in a heart-shaped package, no less. There was no getting away from it all.

That night she and Roque had stayed up together taking care of Meriadoc, she'd felt so close to him. She'd been almost certain that he...

Well, he didn't. And there'd been nothing remotely flirtatious in his manner since then.

They'd finished grading the first trail early in the week, and spent this morning walking a prospective route for the second trail, looking for natural openings through the trees and planning the course of it, the same way they'd done before. And all that time—ever since the Chili Noodle Soup Supper, really—Roque had clearly had something on his mind, something he was hesitant to talk to her about. That wasn't like him. Most of the time, as far as she could tell, he didn't hesitate to say exactly what he was thinking at any given moment. But now, she kept catching him looking at her funny. And just a couple of days ago, he'd gotten a text from someone she was almost certain was her sister Monika. She hadn't seen the content of the text itself, just the name, and only for a fraction of a second before Roque grabbed the phone. That guilty, conscious look on his face had made her feel as if she'd been punched in the stomach.

Would her sister do that to her? Well, why not? Hadn't Susana told her weeks earlier that she wasn't interested in Roque? Maybe Monika had been probing, even then, to see if Susana had a prior claim before going after him herself. And like an idiot, Susana had said no. Small blame to Monika for taking her at her word.

And now here they were at the moment of truth.

Even though she'd been expecting it, she wasn't really ready to hear from Roque's own lips that he was interested in her sister. Would he ask for Susana's permission? Her *blessing*? Or was he just giving her a heads-up because he knew that her feelings for him were a lot less platonic than she'd pretended? Either way, he was clearly steeling himself for something.

"What is it?" she asked, trying to make her voice sound natural.

"I want to take you out tonight...for Valentine's Day."

It took a moment for the words to sort themselves out in her mind.

"You—you want to take me out?" she repeated. "For Valentine's Day?"

"Yes. But I don't want to be pushy. I mean, you are my boss, and you made it clear from the start of our arrangement that you weren't interested in me…romantically." He swallowed. "And I agreed to keep things on a nonromantic level. But my feelings have changed. And I wanted to let you know that, just in case yours have, too. If they haven't, then that's okay. Well, I mean, it's not great, it's not what I want, but I won't be a jerk about it, or blame you for doing exactly what you said you'd do from the start of our…relationship."

He cleared his throat. He was actually nervous.

"So you don't have to worry about that," he went on. "But if your feelings *have* changed—if you want to go out with me—"

"I do." She took a deep breath. "I do want to."

A huge grin spread across his face. "You do? That's great."

She smiled back at him, and for a moment they just stood there smiling at each other.

"So…where do you want to go?" Susana asked.

"To the public dance at Kubicek Hall."

Wow, that was a very specific answer.

"How do you even know about Kubicek Hall?"

"Monika told me. She helped me plan the whole thing. We've been planning it ever since the Chili Noodle Soup Supper."

For a moment Susana was too stunned to think. Then a great swell of happiness bloomed in her chest. Roque wanted *her*. He wanted her enough to do research, to plan.

And Monika was helping him! She hadn't been fooled for a minute by Susana's claims of not being interested in him. She was a wonderful sister.

"Wait!" said Susana. "We can't go to Kubicek's. Their public dances don't start until six. There's no way we could be back in time to feed horses."

"I've already got evening feeding covered. Gillian's going to take care of it. She's done it all by herself the last two times, with me watching, and she didn't make any mistakes. She's ready for a solo run. Her grandfather is going to be here with her, and he says he'll help. And she has the vet's number in case she has any issues."

The next few hours flew by in a blur of delicious anticipation. Susana hurried through her work, then went to the house to shower and dress. It felt so good to use those nice bath things Monika had given her for Christmas, and dig out her pretty hair clips, and put on makeup, and take her time choosing her outfit.

After trying on several possibilities, she settled on a red dress with a flirty ruffle at the hem. The dress was meant to be fingertip length, but on her it came to just above her knees. She pulled on a pair of slip shorts underneath, like she used to when she'd go dancing with her brothers and sisters and cousins back in high school.

By now Roque had gone home to get ready, too. She imagined him in his cramped quarters in the horse trailer, showering and dressing, thinking of her, feeling the same flutter of excitement that she felt.

At exactly ten minutes to five, his sharp knock sounded at her front door. Susana took a last look in the mirror. Her face looked anxious, but her makeup was on point, and her hair hung in perfect glossy spirals down her back.

She opened the door, and there on her front porch was Roque, wearing his black cowboy hat, a solid black T-shirt, dark wash jeans and the caiman belly boots. His dancing boots.

He had his T-shirt in a French tuck that showed off a big belt buckle. A couple of necklaces peeked out from around the collar of his shirt—a cross on a silver chain and a strand of small turquoise beads. It was a young cowboy look—nontraditional, but authentic, and very appealing.

He was holding a wrapped package in one hand and a bouquet in the other— big splashy blossoms, orange and yellow and red.

"Gerbera daisies!" She took the bouquet and breathed in the scent. "Those are my favorite."

"That's what Monika said. She's pretty sharp, that Monika."

"Yes," said Susana. "Yes, she is."

She felt a surge of affection for her sister. How could she ever have believed that Monika was making a move on Roque?

Roque came inside while Susana put the flowers in a stoneware pitcher. He'd been in her house before, more times than she could count, but not like this, all dressed up and looking nervous.

He handed her the package. "Got you a little something," he said.

She opened it to find the dress tack she'd been looking at in the saddle shop, the first time they'd gone to town together. The silver conchos shone bright against the rich leather.

"Roque! Thank you!"

He looked pleased. "Put it on Leda the next time we go riding together," he said.

The hour-long drive covered much of the same territory as the drive to the Chili Noodle Soup Supper. Susana liked the way Roque drove, slouched back in the seat with one long hand resting lazily on the steering wheel, occasionally glancing over at her with a smile.

"Have you ever danced a polka?" Susana asked him.

"Can't say that I have," he replied. "I'm a quick study, though."

"I'm sure you'll pick it up. I can tell you'll be a good dancer, the way you move. We do have a significant height difference, though."

He chuckled. "Yeah, I've noticed. I'm sure we'll figure it out."

They talked about places Roque had lived, the jobs he'd had. He'd once joined the crew of an offshore oil rig based solely on the recommendation of some guy he'd met at a bar the night before. He'd done well there, too, and worked his way up, and was in a position to work his way up even higher.

"So what happened?" Susana asked.

"Well, the company I was keeping left a lot to be desired. Roughnecks are...well, rough. Plus I got tired of being surrounded by nothing but ocean all day and never seeing trees. So I went to work for a logging company. Did that for a few years, then got tired of seeing nothing but trees and cutting them down all day, so I moved back to Jersey City. Went to work doing plumbing for a commercial construction company. That was when I met Layla."

"How long were you together?"

"Eight months." After a brief pause, he said, "I was going to ask her to marry me. I'd bought the ring and everything."

"You never told me that."

"I never told anyone."

She darted a glance at him. He was staring at the road.

"How did you know what ring to get?" she asked.

"Saw it on an open browser when I used her laptop. I thought it was a hint. Apparently it was, but not for me. It wasn't long after that she told me she was engaged to someone else. You know the rest."

Then he said, "Okay, that's enough about my sorry romantic history. Looks like we're almost there."

"Yes, the dance hall is just a couple of blocks away."

Kubicek Hall was a big wooden structure built by Czech and German immigrants in the early 1900s. It had started out as a multipurpose community hall. A place where citizens could conduct business of all kinds, and touring Czech bands could play for public dances. These days, it was used as a venue for private parties—birthdays, reunions, wedding receptions, quinceañeras. The old plank floors had the unmistakable patina of genuine age and use. One end of the building held a bar and grill that served burgers, tacos, kolaches, soft drinks and locally brewed craft beers. The other end was taken up by a wooden stage for the band.

The hall was filled with couples of all ages. Globe lights hung from the ceiling, along with streamers of red hearts. The band was warming up.

"Are you hungry?" Roque asked.

"Not yet. You?"

"No."

Susana's stomach was too fluttery for food. She just wanted to dance.

The band started to play a waltz. Roque gave her a questioning smile and held out his hand. She took it, and he led her out to the floor. She kept her eyes on his broad back, with his arm trailing behind, holding her fingers loosely twined in his.

Then he turned around and took her in his arms.

All at once he was so close, so warm and real, that she could hardly breathe. Around and around they went, gliding along to the triple meter, his arm around her waist, her hand in his. The room spun in endless circles, the white globe lights wheeling past like stars. Susana's heart felt full enough to burst.

She'd learned to dance in this very hall, first by standing on her grandfather's feet, then by practicing with her cousins. There were children here tonight doing the same thing, and older couples who'd clearly been dancing together for decades, and earnest-looking adolescents going at it with a seriousness that left no room for grace.

The height difference turned out to be no trouble at all. Susana was used to dancing with men taller than herself, and Roque was mindful of her shorter steps.

The set list was a mix of German, Czech and Tejano, with some old country in there, too, and some slow numbers where all they did was hold on and sway, with her hand pressed against his chest, engulfed by his. During the slow numbers, he sang along softly. She couldn't hear his Jersey accent, but she could feel his voice resonating through her.

They danced without stopping for the entire first hour, until the band took a break.

"Hungry yet?" Roque asked.

"Famished."

They went to the bar and grill area and ordered burgers and beer. Susana saw aunts and uncles, cousins, and old friends she hadn't seen since before she went away to horsemanship school. She introduced Roque again and again. She was proud of him—of his dancing, his good looks and the way he stayed close to her, attentive but not hovering. She saw the admiring glances he got from other women, but he didn't seem to notice.

Being with him was like something out of a dream. He made her feel precious, cherished, adored. Whenever she spoke, he bent close to her, cupping his hand around his ear to hear her voice in the noisy hall.

Someone laid a hand on her shoulder. "Well, look who's here!"

It was Monika. Susana gave her a fierce hug.

"Having a good Valentine's Day?" Monika asked.

"The best," Susana said.

After eating, they went back to dancing. Around eight o'clock, Gillian sent some pictures of the horses, the cats and Pirko, all looking healthy and happy. Susana showed Roque on her phone. He bent his head so close to hers that his curls tickled her forehead.

The dance ended at nine. They walked out into the big gravel parking lot. The wintry air was deliciously cool after the crowded hall. Susana felt gloriously worn out, her muscles worked in a way she knew she would feel tomorrow, and yet somehow she wasn't tired at all. It had been a long time since she'd been physically challenged by anything other than work. It felt great.

Roque held her hand through the parking lot. He'd held her hand while leading her to the dance floor, but this felt different.

Some big chunks of rough-cut limestone had been set up as parking blocks. Just before they reached the truck, Roque picked Susana up by the waist and set her on top of one.

She wasn't used to seeing him at anything close to eye level, much less from above. Now she was looking down on those black curls, those dark eyes. The harsh overhead light glinted on his hair and threw his face into sharp relief, light and shadow, as if he'd been carved out of stone, like one of the Roman emperors he'd reminded her of the first time she saw him.

He still had his hands on her waist. He leaned in, closing the space between them. She slowly ran her hands up his arms to his shoulders, feeling the rounded hard muscles, the raw power of him.

Then she reached for his hair, took a handful of those curls. They were surprisingly soft.

In one swift motion, he slid his arms around her, tilted up his face and kissed her.

ROQUE HELD SUSANA to him as if he'd never let her go. The shape of her, the taste of her lips, the feel of her fingers moving through his hair in slow circles—everything about her was right, as if she belonged to him.

When at last he drew back, he let out a sigh. "I've been wanting to do that a long time," he said.

"So have I," said Susana.

He picked her up again and set her gently on the ground. "What about the contract?" he asked.

She smiled. "We'll add an amendment."

They didn't talk much on the drive home. Roque was too dazed for conversation. It was enough to feel her hand cupped beneath his on the bench seat. He didn't even want to listen to music. The songs they'd danced to replayed themselves in his head on an endless loop. He could feel a faint echo of motion, as if they were still dancing.

Pirko was curled up on the sofa when

Susana opened the front door. She instantly hopped down and came trotting to meet them, feather tail wagging.

"Yeah, don't try to butter me up," Susana said. "You were naughty. You know you're not supposed to be on the sofa."

Pirko gave her hand a quick lick, then squirted out the door and down the porch steps, where she stopped to look over her shoulder at them, ready to do night check.

"That dog is scary smart," said Roque. "If only we could teach her to drive the truck, she could feed the horses herself."

All the horses looked healthy and happy. The feed barn was shut, with everything put away where it belonged. The empty feed buckets stood in two uneven towers, ready for tomorrow, and the feed truck was parked in its spot.

"Well, would you look at that?" said Roque. "The old place is still standing. Gillian didn't burn it down or leave all the gates open or anything."

"No, she didn't. Everything is squared away."

He gave her a sidewise look. "Kind of makes you think, doesn't it?"

"About what?"

"Possibilities. For more evenings out, pizza runs to Jersey City with your best guy, things like that."

She chuckled and wrapped her arm around his. "It does, actually."

"Really?"

"Yeah. A lot of things seem possible right now. You know, before you came along, I used to look around at this place and see nothing but work to be done. I'd kind of lost my vision. You reminded me of why I got into this business in the first place. You brought back the excitement and magic and fun of it all. Well, that, and you knocked out a lot of the backlog of actual work. You gave me my dream back."

He dropped a kiss on top of her head. "Well, you gave me a place to belong."

"I'm glad you feel that way. Do you ever think about the Hager Ranch?"

He didn't answer right away. "A little. Not as much as I used to."

As a matter of fact, he'd driven by it just the other day, and sat a minute idling his truck at the side of Darnell Road, looking at the entrance gate. A sign hanging from the top read Hager Ranch, with another one underneath that said Since 1856. The signs were a lot more worn than they used to be when Roque would visit for the summer, but the sight of them still stirred a ghost of the excitement he used to feel when Granddad drove the old truck through after picking him up at the airport. It still hurt, but the hurt had shrunk down to a sore spot deep inside that didn't bother him much anymore.

"I'm glad things worked out the way they did," he said. "If I hadn't been living on Mr. Mendoza's lot, Cisco wouldn't have escaped and gone to your place, and I wouldn't have met you."

They took their time walking back to Susana's front door, arms loosely draped around each other. The night was chilly, but not cold, and there was no wind.

"Do you work for Zac tomorrow?" Susana asked.

"Yeah, all day."

"Want to come to dinner after you get off? I'll cook."

His heart surged. She wanted to cook for him? "I'd love to," he said.

She drew closer to him. "You gave me such a nice Valentine's Day surprise. Now it's my turn to treat you."

He kissed her good-night and went out to the truck. His feet were tired, but he felt as if he was walking on air.

CHAPTER SIXTEEN

SUSANA WOKE THE next morning with a vague sensation of leftover happiness, as if she'd just woken from a really good dream. She lay there, eyes shut, savoring the good feeling, and slowly remembered that it wasn't a dream. It was real. Roque had taken her out dancing for Valentine's Day. He'd kissed her in the parking lot of Kubicek Hall and on her front porch. And he was coming over again tonight.

She checked her phone. There was a text from Roque, sent three minutes earlier.

Hey, how's my girl?

A thrill of pleasure shot through her. She lay on her back, smiling up at the words on the screen for a moment before typing, Good morning, cowboy. She sent the text, then added, I miss you.

Almost at the moment she hit Send, another text showed up from him.

I miss you.

They went back and forth that way for a while, until Roque sent a picture of Zac, standing among the studs of a partially framed house and looking grumpy.

My boss says I got to get to work and stop sending goofy love texts to his cousin, the accompanying speech bubble read. I'll see you tonight.

See you, Susana typed, then sat on the edge of her bed, staring at that word *love*. She told herself he didn't mean anything by it. He wasn't one to labor over his words; he generally said the first thing that came into his head without considering every possible implication. But she still liked the sight of the word there on her screen.

The morning passed in a sort of glittery haze of happiness that beautified everything. After morning feeding, she went to H-E-B to get stuff for dinner. It had been a while since she'd really cooked. She'd been living on pizza, convenience food and whatever her mom brought over for her. Now she filled her cart with marked-down Valentine's Day food—one of those sweetheart steaks, along with baby greens and cherry tomatoes for a salad, and russet potatoes for baking. The green onions Roque had planted in the container garden he'd made her were coming up and needed to be thinned. She could snip some of them in place of chives for the potatoes.

Back home, she put the groceries away, started the rib eye marinating and prepped the salad.

Then she did something she hadn't done in years. She took down her old chipped mixing bowl and opened her recipe binder to the yellowed paper with her grandmother's kolache recipe written in faded ink.

Meat and potatoes and pastries, she thought as she dissolved yeast in warm milk and sugar. *I'm feeling domestic about him.*

She added the flour mixture to the proofed yeast and kneaded it into a stiff dough. While the dough was rising, she set the table with a red damask tablecloth and her great-grandmother's Blue Willow china. The kitchen table wasn't big enough for a centerpiece, but she set the white stoneware pitcher of gerbera daisies along the side that butted against the wall.

Everything looked bright and pretty, and the aroma of yeast dough mingled with that of garlic and rosemary from the marinade.

There was nothing more to do to get ready right now, so she went back outside.

It felt strange to be excited and a little nervous about seeing Roque again. What would it be like? They'd had such an easy friendship before last night. They'd fed horses together, built fence together, made trails together. He'd seen her covered with dust and horse hair and bits of hay. Would they still have that good working relationship? They couldn't go back to how things were before, when they were just friends. They couldn't unkiss.

And she didn't want to. She remembered how set she'd been against getting involved with him, how determined she'd been to keep things on a safe level. She was so glad she hadn't followed through.

She had the best of both worlds now. She loved working with him. His twenty-plus hours on the equine center were always the highlight of her week. What would it be like to have him here full-time? Could the place make enough money to support both of them?

Could it make enough to support a family?

A family. It hadn't taken her long to go there. Now that she'd had the thought, it wouldn't go away. She imagined a baby boy with Roque's black curls and laughing dark eyes, learning to ride on Meriadoc like she had when she was little.

Maybe it could work. Business really was booming. Two weeks into February, she already had people calling to schedule summer lessons for their kids and asking if she did a horse camp. Most of the prospective students had been referred by Gillian and her father, who'd apparently had high praise for her abilities as a teacher.

Susana had never held a horse camp before, but judging from how much interest there seemed to be, maybe she should. If she started now, she should have time to put one together. Roque would help.

So many possibilities now. Every day felt like an adventure.

"So?" GILLIAN ASKED when she showed up for her lesson that afternoon. "How was your date?"

Susana felt her cheeks getting warm. "It was good," she said, trying to keep her voice neutral. "Thanks for handling evening feeding."

"Oh, you're welcome. But I didn't do it out of the kindness of my heart, you know. I'm trading work for lessons."

It was fun to hear a little sass from Gillian. She was making terrific progress, and not just in riding. In the weeks since she'd started taking lessons, her whole demeanor had changed. She smiled more and talked without looking as if the words were being dragged out of her, and she and her dad seemed more relaxed around each other.

It was good to see the change in Barrymore, too. He no longer looked sad and alone in his pen. Whenever he heard Kevin's truck coming up the drive, he waited at his gate for Gillian, ears pricked, eager for their ride. It was such a satisfying thing to bring animals and people together and see them help each other.

"Roque's cute," Gillian said. "You two make a good couple."

"Thanks. We've got another date tonight, so you can feed horses by yourself again if you want."

"I'll ask my dad, but it should be fine."

"Good. We'll start a chart just for you, to keep track of your work-for-lessons credits."

Gillian texted Kevin, and he agreed to drive the feed truck for Gillian for evening feeding. After Gillian's lesson was over, Susana left her grooming Barrymore and went to the house to get ready. A hot shower at the end of a long workday always felt good, but having a dinner date to dress up for was even better.

ROQUE PUSHED BACK his seat with a sigh. He felt all comfortable inside, full of steak and potato and beer. The table looked so pretty, with the red cloth and the fancy dishes and the cheerful flowers from yesterday's bouquet. Susana looked even prettier, in that soft pink sweater, her hair held back in a gold clip with red jeweled flowers on it.

"That was delicious," he said.

Susana stacked their dishes. "We're not done yet. I hope you saved room for dessert."

Roque perked up. "Dessert? Oh, dessert goes in a whole separate compartment. I always have room for dessert."

She set down two dainty little blue-and-white dessert plates and brought out—

"Persimmon kolaches!" Roque said.

She smiled. "That's right. In memory of when we first saw each other, as kids, at that Persimmon Festival long ago."

"You must have thought I was such an idiot," he said. "A kid from Jersey in chaps and spurs."

"Actually…" She darted him a quick shy glance. "I had a huge crush on you back then."

He froze with his hand halfway to a kolache. "You did?"

"Mmm-hmm. You were the handsomest

boy I'd ever seen, and so big and confident. I didn't know who you were or where you came from, but I looked for you every year at the Persimmon Festival, and I used to hope I'd randomly run into you somewhere else one day. You were nice, too. You gave me your leftover tickets one year—a strip of seven. You winked at me and told me to go treat myself, on you."

"Did I really? I don't remember that. I don't remember you. I wish I did."

She shrugged. "Well, I was younger than you, and small for my age. I would have just looked like a little girl to you. I *was* a little girl."

"Yeah, I guess so. Do you remember what you got with the tickets?"

Her cheeks turned pink. "I saved them. I still have them."

Roque's heart gave a deep painful throb. "You still *have* them?"

"Yes. That was the last year you came, the last time I saw you, until that day at the feed store."

Roque didn't know what to say. The thought of his callow fourteen-year-old self inspiring that level of devotion in Susana—in anyone—was strangely humbling. He didn't deserve it. Didn't deserve her.

"I'm glad I came back," he said at last.

"I'm glad you came back, too. Don't disappear again."

"Oh, I won't."

He picked up some kolaches. Besides the persimmon ones, there were strawberry and lemon, too. They were like another bouquet there on the china dish. Roque took a bite of the rich, soft, sweet pastry and shut his eyes.

"Mmm! So good. Thank you for doing all this."

"You're welcome. So what do you think about horse camp? Can we do it? Do we have time to pull it together?"

"I don't see why not. We can start promoting it in town right away. Make some posters, put them up at the feed store, Darcy's Hardware, Lalo's Kitchen, the donut shop, the Cocina de Pecarí."

"We need to figure out dates and a daily schedule before we advertise."

They talked and planned over their kolaches, and before long they had a tentative schedule worked out. Then they did night check together, and Susana walked Roque to his truck and kissed him goodnight.

Roque drove home in a daze, with a ziptop bag of kolaches on the bench seat behind him. Everything was so good right now—with Susana, with the horses, with everything. His entire world had turned around. Two months ago, he never could have guessed that he could be so happy.

Inside his trailer, he set the bag of kolaches on top of his microwave and took off his boots. He was just pulling his shirt off when his phone went off with a call from an unknown number.

He answered. "Hello?"

"Hello, Roque?"

Roque froze. "Yeah," he said. "Who's this?"

But he already knew. He knew that voice. It couldn't be. But it was.

"This is your cousin Dirk. If you're not busy right now, I'd like to get together and have a little talk."

CHAPTER SEVENTEEN

"So let me get this straight," said Roque. "You want to start an internship program for teaching country skills to people who are new to country life. And you want me to help you run that program."

Dirk took another swallow of his beer. "That's about the size of it, yeah."

Roque didn't know what to say. It felt strange enough, sitting here in a booth at Tito's Bar, drinking beer with the man who'd been aggressively shunning him for the past year. Dirk's words added a whole other layer of unreality.

"Why?" asked Roque. "You've made it pretty clear that you don't like newcomers. Especially me."

The corners of Dirk's mouth barely edged up in the hint of a smile. "Well, let's just say I've had a change of perspective. Look, I'm not thrilled about old family ranches being broken up and sold off. But it's happening, whether I like it or not. Long and short of it is, the new folks are here to stay. They've got to learn to get along, and the old-timers like myself have got to learn to get along with them. Some of them aren't half bad. They just don't know what they're doing. They need help. Not just with the skills, although that's a big part of it, but with the whole social end of things. They need to learn to understand and respect the way of life around here and the people who live it." Dirk shot Roque an icy blue glance. "Sort of like what Susana Vrba's been teaching you."

Roque smiled. "You heard about that, did you?"

"Oh, yeah. The whole town's been watching your every move since you first showed up. Some of the guys even set up a betting pool on how long you'd last."

Roque started to ask if Dirk had bought in to the pool, then decided he didn't really want to know.

"So what exactly do you have in mind for this internship program?" he asked.

"It's still in the planning stages, but

we've got some ideas. Horsemanship, cattle, poultry. Basic carpentry. Pasture management. Hat etiquette. That sort of thing. Maybe some courses on sewing and home canning."

Roque nodded. "So where would I fit in?"

"Well, you're not a bad horseman, and you were always good with a rope. With Granddad gone, I've been running myself ragged doing the work of two men on the ranch. It'll take a while before the interns pull their own weight. I could use a relatively experienced cowboy on the place."

"You're offering me an actual job?"

"I am. So what do you say? You want in?"

Did he want in? Of course he wanted in. But there was something he needed to know first.

Roque cleared his throat. "Can I ask you something?"

Dirk gave him a wary look. "Shoot."

"Why'd you always hate me so much? I mean, I get that I was probably an annoying kid, but was I really *that* bad?"

Dirk took so long to answer that Roque started to think he wasn't going to at all.

Finally he said, "I guess the truth is, I was jealous. I'd been an only son and only grandson my whole life, and now suddenly here was Granddad making a big fuss over some new kid—buying you those spurs and chaps, teaching you to rope, taking you with him everywhere, and making me look after you whenever he wasn't around to do it himself. It was like I suddenly got demoted to a hired hand, only without the pay. And it didn't help that you were pretty good at riding and roping. Then after Granddad passed—well, I wasn't thrilled about him giving you his horse, and losing that cash was rough on the ranch. Plus I had my own stuff going on then, with my marriage falling apart and—" He set his beer down. "Anyhow. Do you want in, or don't you?"

"Yeah," said Roque. "Yeah, I want in."

Dirk gave him a quick nod. "Good. I don't have a whole lot of family left, and I reckon you're the closest thing to a brother I'm ever going to have."

Roque's throat swelled up, and his eyes

stung. Dirk looked away, pretending not to notice.

Once Roque had his face under control, they kicked around some ideas for how to set up the internship. Apparently Roque wasn't the first person Dirk had talked it over with.

"You remember Alex Reyes," he said. "His grandfather owned the place next to ours. It's his now. And Miss Ida, over on Petty Road—you know, the lady that kept all the chickens."

"Yeah, I remember both of them. Alex is a little younger than you, right? You and he were always friends. And Miss Ida was always giving away food."

Dirk chuckled. "Still is."

It felt good, reminiscing, talking about people they both knew. As if Roque had a history there. As if he belonged.

"Some of the new neighbors are going to help with the teaching end of things," Dirk said. "They aren't all tenderfoots. Some of them already have country skills. Walt Franklin—you wouldn't know him, he's not from around here, but he knew my dad way back. He bought a place near me.

He knows about welding and engine repair and how to raise and butcher hogs. Then there's Macy. Macy Reinalda."

Something in Dirk's voice caught Roque's attention.

"She's from New York, but she's a fully naturalized Texan now," Dirk went on. "She knows all kinds of stuff—canning, sewing, knitting, quilting. Matter of fact, this whole internship thing was her idea."

"I see," said Roque. "Would this Macy have anything to do with your change of heart toward newcomers?"

Dirk smiled, a full-on smile this time. "Maybe. And she's right. The world is changing. Farming and ranching are changing. The operations that survive are going to have to come to terms with that and figure out a way forward."

Roque nodded and took a swallow of his beer.

"How's Cisco?" Dirk asked.

"He's good. I'm boarding him at Susana's place now. I guess you heard that, too."

"Yeah. She's a real sweetheart, Susana

is, and a heck of a horsewoman. Used to work for Granddad, you know."

"Yeah, she told me."

He wanted to say more about Susana, but he suddenly felt tongue-tied. What exactly was the status of his relationship with her? They'd been on three dates, if you counted the Chili Noodle Soup Supper, which Roque was inclined to do. Was she his girlfriend now? He was almost certain she was, but he figured he'd better run that by her before spouting off to someone else about it.

"How's Ava?" he asked.

"Spunky as ever and traveling the world."

"When you talk to her next, tell her Cousin Rocky said hey."

"I'll do that. Are you still living in that old horse trailer of Juan Mendoza's?"

"Sure am."

Dirk shook his head. "You've got grit, I'll give you that. How'd you make out during the Snowpocalypse?"

"Fine, other than being bored out of my mind. My pipes didn't freeze, which is more than a lot of folks can say."

"Isn't that the truth," Dirk grumbled.

"Mine all froze up, plus half a pecan tree fell through my roof."

"What, one of those big old pecan trees at the farmhouse?"

"Yep. Had to replace the roof, and half the windows and drywall, and refinish the hardwood floors, and rebuild the front porch. I just finished getting the place back into shape. You ought to come over and see it."

"Thanks, I'd like that."

Dirk thought a little longer. "In fact, why don't you hitch up your horse trailer, and haul it back to the ranch, and move in?"

"You mean set up Mr. Mendoza's horse trailer on the ranch and live in it there?"

"No, genius. I mean move into the house. It's all fixed up now and I've got a spare room. If you're going to be working on the ranch, you might as well live there, too."

SUSANA HAD BEEN researching horse camps all morning. Her mind was filled to bursting with ideas and plans. She'd already printed some reproducible registration forms and some worksheets for teaching horse anatomy and the parts of a Western saddle. Now she was debating whether she ought to do a full-day camp her first year or just a half-day to start. The problem with an all-day camp was that the afternoons got so hot. She and her brothers and sisters used to play outside in the Texas summer, but everyone said that today's youth were a softer set. She didn't want the kids complaining about the heat, much less actually stroking out. If she had a nice big barn for the campers to come into after lunch, out of the sun, for tack work and some classroom-type instruction—

But she didn't, so she'd have to start with half a day for now. She looked at the tentative schedule she'd penciled in with Roque's help. Breakfast, horsemanship, grooming, trail ride, barn chores, lunch. They ought to get as early a start as possible to take advantage of the coolest part of the day—say, seven in the morning. The campers could work their way through different levels of achievement and get awarded T-shirts at the end, maybe with a nice logo on them. The logo could go on the posters, too. Maybe she could get a photographer to come out and take some pictures of the horses and the trails to use for promotional materials.

She thought again of the big barn she didn't have. If there *was* a way for her to offer afternoon hours, she could charge more. Could she maybe bring the campers inside the house? That would depend on how many signed up. Her living room wasn't very big. Could she possibly set up a sort of classroom in the arena, or under a canopy? Or maybe the afternoon heat wasn't as big a deal as she was making it out to be. At this point, she just didn't know anymore.

What she really needed was to talk the whole thing over with Roque. He was her best brainstorming and planning partner. Somehow her ideas always seemed to jell better when he was around.

Her phone rang. She looked at the screen. It was Curt calling.

"Curt! Hey, how are you? How's Contessa? Is she settling into her new home?"

"Hey, Susana. Contessa's great. Reveling in her new pasture, and getting acquainted with a retired racehorse and a neighbor's mule."

"Glad to hear it. So what's up?"

"Well, I saw Roque the other day at Lalo's Kitchen, and he said something interesting. Something about an Iraq war veteran who's started riding out at your place. Roque said the guy is blind?"

"That's right."

"How does that work, exactly?"

"It's actually pretty simple. Garrett goes on trail rides with a group. The horses are all very seasoned and steady. Garrett rides a gelding called Clem, who's friends with another horse named Ajax. We always have Ajax right in front of Clem, so Clem's with a horse he knows and is comfortable with. Once they're on the trail, there's only one way to go, and the horses just follow each other. Pretty much all Garrett has to do is hold on and keep his seat. It helps that he already knew how to ride before he lost his sight. Whenever there's an incline coming up, or an obstacle that Garrett needs to be aware of, like a low-hanging branch, the rider ahead of him tells him, and he adjusts."

"Back up a minute. You say Ajax and Clem are *friends*?"

"That's right. They live in the same pen together, too. They worked at the same ranch together for years before they came to me. It gives them a bond. Whenever any of my horses have a shared prior history and get along well with each other, it makes sense to honor that relationship and keep them together as much as possible. It just makes things go smoother."

Curt chuckled. "I guess it would. You really know your stuff, don't you?"

"I had good teachers," Susana said.

Curt was silent a moment, then went on, "Susana, have you ever considered hosting a therapeutic riding operation?"

"No."

"Would you be willing to consider it?"

"I... I don't know. I've heard of programs like that, of course. Some people I met at horsemanship school are involved in it. But I'm not really trained for it or set up for it out here."

"What if I took care of that? What if I found someone who was trained, or paid for you to get training, and fronted the money for any special equipment you'd need? I'd underwrite the whole program and make sure you received fair compensation."

"I, uh… Wow. I don't know what to say, Curt. That's a lot to think about."

"I know it is. But these programs can do a lot of good with veterans and other trauma survivors."

"I'm sure they can. But there are other people who are already doing things like that. Wouldn't it make more sense for you to invest in them?"

"It might. But I invest in people, and I'd rather work with you. I know you and trust you. The whole community trusts you. Everyone knows you're a hard worker with a lot of integrity. I wouldn't have any qualms about providing the financial backing for a program like this if you were at the helm."

Susana's head spun. She hadn't even finalized plans for horse camp yet, and here was a whole new opportunity.

"You don't have to give me an answer today," said Curt. "I'm not sure how the nuts and bolts of the thing would work or if it would be feasible at all. I just wanted to know if you had enough interest in the idea for me to pursue it."

Susana thought fast. If even half the things she was already planning came to fruition, she was going to have a lot of irons in the fire. But she wasn't on her own anymore. She had Roque now. And this was a chance to really help people, to bring comfort and healing to people who needed them.

"It does sound worth pursuing," she said. "If you want to look into it, I'll be interested to hear what you find out."

"I'm glad to hear that." He paused a moment, then said, "I had a brother who fought in Iraq. He, uh, he didn't adjust very well after he came back home. He's gone now, and there's nothing more I can do for him, but if I can help others like him…"

He trailed off.

"Yes," Susana said. "Thank you for wanting me to be part of that."

After she hung up with Curt, Susana sat there a moment, staring at her phone. She had to tell Roque about this.

Then her phone lit up with a text from him.

OK if I come over? I've got news.

She smiled. Yes. I have news, too. Come as soon as you can.

She went outside to meet him. The grass was still yellow and dry, and the live oaks were looking more like dead oaks with their brown leaves, but the air was mild, and the February day felt like spring. In the container garden Roque had planted for her, little crumpled lettuce leaves were coming up, and spinach and radishes, too.

He arrived within a few minutes, parked his truck and hurried up the walkway in that eager long-legged stride. When he reached Susana, he took her in his arms and spun her around.

"Hey there! How's my girl?"

"Better than ever, now that you're here," she said and kissed him.

He held her to him for a long moment before gently setting her down. "You'll never guess who called me last night."

At this point, with all the surprising things that had been happening, she wouldn't even venture to try.

Fortunately, he didn't wait for her to

guess. The news burst out of him. "Dirk! It was Dirk. He said he had something to talk over with me, so we met at Tito's for a beer. Susana, he wants me to come work for him."

"Come work for him?" Susana repeated.

Roque's face shone with excitement. "On the Hager Ranch. Isn't that amazing? Apparently he's had a complete change of heart about all the newcomers moving to this area. Get this. He wants to start an internship program to teach them every-thing they need to know about living in the country, and he wants me to help!"

"Internship?" she said, echoing him again. She couldn't get her mind in gear to come up with any words of her own.

"Yeah! You know how Granddad and Dirk used to lease the old Masterson place and run their cattle on it, but then the Mas-tersons sold their land to developers?"

"Yes, I know," Susana said. Of course she knew. She was the one who'd told *him* that.

"Well, the developers carved the land into lots, twenty to a hundred acres, and sold them to people who wanted to live in the country. The biggest lot is on this low-land area that's really good for hay. Dirk is going to lease it from the owners and keep on grazing cattle and growing hay there. The owners will get to keep their ag exemption, and Dirk gets enough hay for his own herds, plus maybe enough to sell in a good year. Everyone wins! And Dirk's already started working with another rancher, and other folks he knows who have country skills, to set up lessons. He wants to cover riding, roping, working cattle, raising chickens, all kinds of stuff. The newcomers get to learn how to do things, and the ranchers get some free labor out of the deal. Isn't that great?"

"It sounds like a lot of work."

He actually laughed, as if that was icing on the cake. "I know, right? There's so much to figure out and do."

He went on about it for a while. He didn't seem to notice how quiet Susana was being. She'd been waiting to tell him her own news about Curt's therapeutic riding idea, and talk some more about horse camp, but now all her excitement was leaking out like air from a pricked balloon.

"Are you going to do it?" she asked.

Silly question, but she had to hear him say it.

"Sure, I'm going to do it! This is exactly what I wanted."

"It'll be a big commitment, time-wise," she said.

"Yeah, it will. I'll have to give Zac notice, obviously. He's been a good boss, and I appreciate him giving me work when no one else would, but he won't have any problem replacing me."

"That's true, I guess. But it won't be so easy for me."

His head tilted. "Wait a second. You don't think I'd give up working here, do you?"

"I don't see how you could possibly keep it up, and work at the ranch, and help Dirk with his internship program."

"It's a lot, I know. But I'll figure it out. You'll see."

He looked so sure of himself, just like when he'd said he could get the chainsaw running again, and the dozer. She wanted to believe him. But he couldn't do it all. He couldn't keep pulling a rabbit out of a hat.

"How?" she asked. "Energy and enthusiasm can only accomplish so much. There are limits, actual physical limits to what people can do, Roque. There's a set number of hours in the day."

He shrugged. "So I work forty hours a week for Dirk and twenty hours here, like we agreed. That's doable."

Except that he didn't work just twenty hours a week at Susana's place. He never had. For the past month, he'd been averaging thirty-plus. Which would be fine if it were just a bunch of onetime chores he was knocking out for her and nothing else, but it wasn't. He'd set things in motion that couldn't be maintained without his help. All the extra business he'd brought in—extra clients, extra students—it all meant a lot more work. As for horse camp and therapeutic riding, could she even get them off the ground without him?

It wasn't as if he'd ever made her any promises—other than twenty hours of work a week, which he'd exceeded right from the start. And it wasn't as if she hadn't known his endgame. She'd said it herself. *Come work for me, and learn from me, and maybe Dirk will take notice of you.* Well, that was exactly what had happened. Her strategy had succeeded.

But she didn't say any of that. She just said, "There won't be any need for you to work your twenty hours a week here anymore, because Cisco won't be here. He'll be back at the Hager Ranch with you."

Roque rubbed his beard. "Oh. Right. I guess I hadn't thought that far out yet. This is all still so new."

"Yes. And I know how much you love whatever's new."

She hadn't meant to say that part out loud. But it was true. He was bored here, now that things were finally coming together, and ready for a new challenge. Just like all those times when he'd quit a job to move across the country and do something else.

Roque's smile froze, then faded away. He looked as if she'd slapped him.

"You don't believe me," he said. "You think I won't follow through. You think I don't have it in me to do what I say."

"What else can I think, Roque? I'm thankful for everything you've done here, but you've generated so much new business that I can't do all the work by myself anymore. I had a hard enough time doing it to begin with."

"I'll still come," he said.

"What for?" she asked.

Roque held his hands out. "For you!"

He stood there, eyes wide, with that stricken look on his face. She wanted to go to him and let him fold her in his arms and tell her everything would be all right. She wanted to believe that he really cared about her. But she'd only be setting herself up for a fall.

"Let's be realistic," she said. "Our arrangement was always month to month, subject to being ended at any time by either party."

His hands fell to his sides. "Our *arrangement*? What about us? You're not just a contract to me, Susana!"

She didn't answer right away. Only a day earlier, she'd been allowing herself to dream about the future, wondering if the equine center could support both of them—could support a *family*. She cringed at the memory. What an idiot she'd been.

"We went out a few times. We kissed. And when I asked if you still thought about the Hager Ranch, you said you were glad things worked out the way they did, because otherwise you wouldn't have met me. But the second Dirk called, you went running."

His mouth pressed itself into a grim line. "Are you giving me an ultimatum?" he asked.

"No. I'm just calling it like I see it. If this is the end, better to say so at once and be done with it. I won't be crowded out a little at a time. I won't watch you get more and more excited about the Hager Ranch, the way you once were about my place, showing up here less and less often, but always with a good excuse, and finally not coming at all anymore."

"Wow," Roque said quietly. "So that's what you think of me. That I'm just a kid with a shiny new toy. That I'm like one of those horse owners who send in their checks every month but never come to visit. If that's all I am, then I guess I'm no great loss."

His face blurred. She blinked rapidly,

then said, "Let me know when you want to pick up Cisco and his tack."

"Okay," he said. She'd never heard him sound so flat and calm.

And then he was gone.

CHAPTER EIGHTEEN

THE STONE HOUSE on the Hager Ranch looked familiar and strange at the same time. The old limestone siding was as mellow as Roque remembered, but the front porch was bright with new lumber. Inside, the fireplace was the same, but the hardwood floors had a new glow and gloss to them, and the drywall was new and freshly painted. The built-in china cabinet was in the same spot as before, but Dirk had rebuilt it. The boxy armchair Dirk was sitting in looked like the one Granddad used to have, but with different fabric.

Also, the entire house seemed to have shrunk.

"How did Nonna and Granddad ever fit three grandkids in here?" he asked Dirk "I remember it being this huge gracious house, but this place is tiny!"

Dirk chuckled. "Yeah, I don't know.

felt the same way when I first got back from Iraq. Like, what happened to the rest of the house? I did get a lot of old junk cleared out of here recently, which helped a lot space-wise, but I'm thinking about maybe adding on one day, in case... Well, you know."

Roque followed Dirk's gaze across the room to Macy, who was pouring coffee in the kitchen while Taffy, Dirk's orange kitten, climbed up the legs of her skinny jeans.

"Ooh," Roque said in a low voice. "You thinking about popping the question?"

Dirk gave him a hint of a smile. "It's early days yet, but—yeah, I am."

"Good for you," Roque said. "She seems really great."

Macy did seem great. Serious and super smart, quiet and capable, with a lot of New York in her voice and a lot of Texas in her soul. Roque liked her, and he was happy for them both, but thinking about them maybe getting married made him feel hollow inside.

Not just hollow. There was an actual pain in his chest, like the old bullet wound, but deeper. This one went all the way to his heart.

He didn't understand what had happened. He'd thought things were going great between Susana and himself. He'd just started allowing himself to imagine a future where he wasn't alone, and now...

"I'm sorry, what was that?" he asked, dimly aware that Dirk had been talking to him.

"I was just saying that once you move Cisco over, we'll saddle up him and Monte and go for a ride," Dirk said. "The pastures are configured about the same as when you were here last, but after eighteen years, I reckon you could use a refresher on how everything's laid out. I also want to show you where to cross the creek to get to Macy's place, and from there to the acreage where we're going to raise hay. There's a gate that opens onto Alex's property, too. Our grandfathers put it in, and it's come in handy a lot of times. We'll make an afternoon of it and ride over the whole ranch."

"I'd like that," said Roque, trying to

sound more enthusiastic than he felt. Riding the property with Dirk as an equal—or at least as a respected fellow worker—was a dream come true. But the shine had worn off the dream, somehow.

Macy set her mug on the coffee table and joined Dirk in the armchair. It was a tight fit, but she was slender enough to make it work.

"Did you ask him about Susana?" she asked Dirk.

Roque's heart gave a painful jolt. "Ask me what about Susana?"

"About her teaching horseback riding to some of our interns," said Dirk.

"I figured you'd handle that yourself," said Roque.

Dirk chuckled. "So did I, until I tried it. There's this one kid, Tim, who really wants to learn. Our first and only lesson didn't go so great. I know Granddad taught you, and I guess he taught me, though I started so young that I don't remember actually learning. But apparently knowing how to do something yourself doesn't necessarily translate into being able to teach someone else. So naturally I thought of Susana. I've heard a lot of good things about her as a teacher. Do you think she's interested in taking on any new students right now?"

"Um, I don't know. She's got a lot going on, with all her new clients, and she's thinking of doing a horse camp this summer."

"Maybe you could run it by her and see what she thinks."

Roque rubbed the back of his neck. "Actually... Susana and I got a little cross with each other earlier today."

It was something Granddad used to say, that someone got cross with someone else. Roque was a little surprised to hear the words coming out of his own mouth.

"Oh?" said Dirk. "I'm sorry to hear that."

"Yeah, the whole thing kind of blindsided me. I'm not real sure what happened or why."

Dirk squinted at him. "Does it have anything to do with you coming to work for me?"

"More or less, yeah."

"So are the two of you…together?"

"Not anymore. I'm not sure we ever were."

He told them as much of the conversation as he could remember. "It isn't fair," he said. "I don't know why she had to assume I would flake out on her all of a sudden, just because I got a job here. I don't see why it has to be an either-or."

Dirk frowned in thought. "I get where she's coming from. Running a ranch is a lot of work."

"You don't think I can do both?" Roque asked.

"I'm just saying it's a valid concern."

"Maybe she wants you more than part-time," said Macy. "Or maybe she just wants to be number one with you."

Roque thought about that. "I don't want to choose."

"It sounds like you might have to," said Macy. "Saying yes to one thing always means saying no to something else."

"Look," said Dirk, "why don't you take some time to decide? I don't want to pressure you into doing something you'll regret."

Roque looked out the window. The

Hager Ranch stretched before him, the wonderland of his boyhood, and the dream that had kept him going after being shot, and driven him eighteen hundred miles to make it come true. He wanted to be a part of this place and work side by side with Dirk.

But not if it meant losing Susana. He'd put down roots with her and couldn't bear to rip them up.

He set his mug down and looked Dirk in the eye. "Thank you for offering me a place here, Dirk. You have no idea how much it means to me. But Susana is the one who took me in and sorted me out when no one else would give me the time of day. I belong with her now. I think— I think maybe I'm in love with her. No. I *am* in love with her."

"All right, then," said Dirk. "You'd better go tell her so."

Dirk and Macy walked Roque to the door. He stepped outside and put his hat on.

Dirk held out a hand. Roque gripped it tight.

"Don't be a stranger," said Dirk. "Whether you work for me or not, you're family now."

"Thanks," Roque said.

He got in his truck and drove away.

CHAPTER NINETEEN

SUSANA LUGGED LEDA'S saddle out of the feed barn and heaved it onto the fence rail, then stood a moment, staring at the building's open door. Why did she call it a feed barn, anyway? It wasn't a feed barn, and the saddle rack wasn't a tack room. The whole thing wasn't anything more than a cheaply made portable storage building, smaller than a walk-in closet, and that was all it would ever be.

It was high time she faced some hard facts. She'd never be able to afford a raised center aisle barn with twelve stalls and a wash station and separate feed and tack rooms and all that. Who was she kidding? It was never going to happen. No amount of frugality and hard work could change the high price of feed or put hard capital in her hand. That was the truth, and it didn't do any good to pretend otherwise.

For a while, Roque had made her believe she could have her dream barn, her dream facility, her dream everything. He could make her believe anything. Not just because he was a good talker, although he was, but because of his ability to get things done—whether it was fixing machinery, or clearing brush, or making one of his deals. It was like magic.

But now he was gone, and Susana was on her own again.

She put a halter and lead rope on Leda, tied her to the fence and started going over her coat with the currycomb.

Should she try to find another hired man? It wasn't out of the question. Between the trail rides and the new boarders, the place was bringing in a lot more money now. And with all the extra work that went along with that, she really needed the help. She couldn't do it all on her own anymore. She'd barely managed to keep afloat before Roque had come along.

But she didn't want another hired hand. She wanted a partner.

She wanted Roque.

Well, she couldn't have him. He was

off to the Hager Ranch—which was what *he'd* wanted all along. And now Susana would have to start over with someone else. And unless that person also wanted a work-for-board barter arrangement, *and* had a tireless capacity for work in addition to immense personal charm, *and* was willing to put in a lot more than twenty hours a week no matter what the contract said, she was going to lose ground. She'd have to pay wages, which would cut into those nice profits Roque had helped to bring in.

She saddled Leda and got on, then headed for the trail. Pirko trotted along behind her like a good trail dog.

The heart-shaped hollow in the pecan tree at the trail head mocked her feelings. Sweetheart Trail? More like Heartbreak Path.

Well, it was her own fault for thinking he was finally putting down some roots, here, with her. For allowing herself to envision him as a permanent part of her life.

Now that the trail was finished and in use, Susana had to check it regularly to make sure it was in good shape. Garrett was scheduled to ride tomorrow, and Susana didn't want any stray branches blocking the trail or hanging down where he'd have to dodge them or else get smacked in the face.

Sure enough, there was a fairly stout oak branch that had detached from its trunk and started to fall, only to get caught in other branches on the way down. Now the tip of it was hanging down right at face-smacking level.

Susana halted Leda underneath the branch. If Roque were here, he'd reach up from Cisco's saddle, pull the branch down and toss it away with hardly any effort at all, but it was another matter when you were barely five feet tall.

Well, she'd just have to get used to doing things on her own again.

She struggled with the branch for a few minutes before it finally sprang free in a litter of falling twigs and a rustle of dry leaves. Susana's weight shifted, startling Leda, who shied a little. Leda was skittish already today. Probably she could sense Susana's mood.

Susana tossed the branch onto the side of the trail and kept going.

This really was a beautiful trail, and it would look even better come spring. Every inch of it reminded her of Roque. She remembered every spot where the two of them had stopped to debate its course. She half expected to see him around the next turn, working the chainsaw, his lips moving to the words of whatever country song he was singing at the moment, in spite of the fact that no one, not even himself, could hear him over the chainsaw's racket.

The trees gave way to the relatively open space, showing the part of the property where she and Roque had talked about putting a hay field one day. A big bank of dark cloud was massing up to the Northeast. It hadn't been there when she'd set out on her ride—or if it had, she'd been too distracted to notice. There was an uplift in the wind, too, with the trees showing the underside of their leaves. No wonder Leda was nervous. The mare lifted her head and snuffled the air. So did Pirko.

Should they head back? Susana didn't want to get caught in a downpour, but the clouds were still a good distance away.

She decided she still had time to finish the trail. Anyway, she had to. She was booked solid tomorrow and wouldn't have another chance to clear the trail before Garrett's ride.

There was even some satisfaction to be had in the dark sky and the ominous feeling in the air. The pretty springlike morning had been like a personal insult after Roque had left.

The worst part was that she'd known the danger all along of growing close to this attractive, charismatic man, and she'd done it anyway. He'd barged right into her heart in his pushy Yankee way, and instead of resisting, she'd welcomed him. Now he was gone, leaving behind a big empty space that hadn't been there before, or if it had, she hadn't known any better.

A low rumble of thunder sounded off to the Northeast, like a sheet of tin being shaken out in the wind.

Then lightning flashed, followed closely by a loud crack surprisingly close by. It startled Susana, and it startled Leda even more. The mare let out a high frightened neigh. The world spun by in a confused blur of motion, rushed up to meet her and exploded in pain.

So much pain. It radiated from her right shoulder into her chest and arm and through her entire body. Susana hadn't known it was possible to hurt that much. She'd taken falls from horses before, lots of times, but never like this.

At first she couldn't breathe. Then she managed to roll onto her back and lay there a moment, dazed, staring up at the roiling clouds in a rapidly darkening sky.

Suddenly, Pirko was there, licking her on the face and whining. Susana appreciated the sentiment, though it wasn't of much practical value.

And it didn't last long. Pirko ran off barking, the sound trailing away into silence.

So much for her loyal dog.

Something warm and wet trickled down her cheek. She spat out a mouthful of dirt. A fresh wave of pain washed over her, and she shut her eyes.

"SUSANA? CAN YOU hear me? Susana, please."

It was Roque's voice, but she'd never

heard him sound like that before. Scared, almost panicky.

She opened her eyes and saw him bending over her, backlit by a weird greenish glow in the sky.

"Oh, thank God," he murmured. "Can you move? Actually, forget that. Don't try to move. Your spine could be hurt. I'm calling an ambulance."

"Oh no you're not," she tried to say, but it came out as a wordless groan.

He took out his phone and started punching in numbers. Was he out of his mind? She couldn't afford an ambulance. She reached for the phone—

Her shoulder flared with a fresh surge of pain. She screamed.

"Don't move!" Roque said again.

Pirko danced around nearby, frantic with worry. Roque turned to her and said sharply, "Pirko, sit!"

Pirko sat, trembling and whining.

Susana ground her teeth, braced herself and with a tremendous effort made it to a sitting position. It hurt, but it also showed—to her own satisfaction, at least—that there was nothing wrong with her spine.

She took Roque's hand. "Help me up," she said.

Somehow she made it to her feet. She was gasping with pain by now.

Roque held on to her. "Okay, okay," he said. "Let's see if we can make it to my truck and I'll drive you to the emergency room."

"No ER," she said. "Urgent care."

"Okay, fine. Can you walk? Should I carry you? Where are you hurt?"

"It's my shoulder," she said. "Don't try to pick me up. Just help me walk."

They made their way slowly back up the trail, with Pirko looping ahead of them and back again, taking at least ten steps to every one of theirs. Susana wished she would be still. The whole world was tilting and whirling. It made her stomach hurt. She shut her eyes, but that only made the dizziness worse.

Finally, they reached the end of the lane. Leda was standing alongside the feed barn, head lowered and tail tucked.

"I'll bring my truck over so you don't have to walk anymore," said Roque.

"Take care of Leda first," said Susana.

He gave her a pained look.

"Take care of her," she said again. "I've made it this far. It won't kill me to wait another five minutes."

She leaned against the feed barn wall, clutching the arm of her hurt shoulder, while Roque unsaddled Leda at breakneck pace and then led her back to her pasture. Pirko sat right by Susana the whole time, resting her rump on Susana's boot, as if to anchor her in place.

Susana's stomach was not in good shape. She felt as if she were about to throw up, and if there was one thing she did not want to do right now, it was throw up. She stared hard at a fence post, trying to make the world stop whirling and mind-over-matter her way out of the nausea.

It didn't work. She threw up. Her shoulder shrieked in pain. Somehow she ended up on her knees. And then Roque was there, holding her, smoothing her hair back, murmuring soothing sounds to her. She emptied her stomach, closed her eyes and took some deep shuddering breaths.

The next thing she knew, she was in Roque's truck, without any memory of how she'd gotten there, lying on her left side with the seat belt somehow buckled around her hips.

"Is this a dream?" she heard herself ask.

"No, baby," said Roque. "This is real. You're hurt and I'm taking you to the doctor."

He'd never called her baby before. She liked it.

"It's raining," she said.

"Yes, it is," said Roque. "We need the rain, but I hope it'll wait until we get where we're going before it really lets loose."

Then suddenly the two of them were in some sort of examining room.

"How do they keep changing the scenery so fast?" Susana asked.

Roque took her left hand. "We're at urgent care, baby. I drove you here, remember?"

His head was tilted to one side and his forehead was all wrinkled up. He looked like a worried puppy dog.

"You're adorable," she said.

He smiled a little. "Well, thanks. You're pretty good-looking yourself."

He started to raise her hand to his face,

seemed to think better of it and bent down to kiss it instead. She liked the feel of his beard tickling her skin.

Then a ripple of panic went through her.

"What about the horses?" she asked.

"The horses are fine," said Roque. "The rain is supposed to let up for a while this evening, and when it does, Gillian will go feed them."

"Who?"

His face got worried again. "Gillian. Gillian Fox. You remember her."

Susana started shaking her head, then stopped because it hurt too much. Was he making stuff up?

And why was he holding her hand?

"Are we together?" she asked. "You and me?"

Now he looked a little sick. "You don't remember that either?"

"No. Did we get together?"

"Um…yeah. We got together. We went out for Valentine's Day. Does that ring a bell?"

"No. Where did we go?"

"Out dancing. I learned to polka."

"Did you really?" Wow. That must have

been something. "I wish I could remember," she said.

"Maybe you will. So, uh, what do you think, how do you feel, about us getting together?"

"I like it. I told Monika I didn't like you that way, but I lied."

Something—not a memory exactly, but a cold feeling of dread—came over her.

"Wait," she said. "Are you going away?"

He gripped her hand tight. "No, baby. I'm not going anywhere. I'm staying right here for as long as you want me."

Eventually, things stopped happening in random, disconnected blocks and started following a reasonable sequence. Several tests and examinations later, Susana had a diagnosis: a broken collarbone, multiple cuts and contusions, and a Grade Three concussion.

Susana had to stay quiet and still, the doctor said. It would take her at least three weeks to recover from the concussion alone, longer for the collarbone. No horseback riding until her symptoms had cleared up completely. No strenuous activity of any kind.

She stared at the doctor in horror.

"I can't wait that long," she said. "I have a business to run. I can't take off a whole month. Everything will fall apart."

"I understand that it's a long time to take off," the doctor said. "But the effects of a concussion are cumulative. If you go back to your normal activities without giving your brain a chance to heal, you'll exacerbate the injury."

"No no no no no. You don't understand. I have horses to take care of. I can't sit around resting for a whole *month*!"

Susana's eyes burned, her throat got tight and she heard a roaring in her ears. Tears spilled down her cheeks. This was exactly what she was always afraid would happen. That nagging fear, whispering in the back of her mind. What if she got hurt? Who would take care of the horses then? And now she'd gone and done it. So many animals depending on her, and she'd let them down.

And then Roque was there, bending down to get his face in front of hers. He didn't look worried now. He looked fierce.

"Susana! Listen to me. It isn't all up to you, okay? You aren't the only person in the world who is capable of feeding those horses, and you aren't the only one who cares about them. You've got a whole community of people who are ready to help you, and I'm at the top of the list. All you have to do is rest and get better. I'm going to take care of you now."

"You're sure you're not going away?"

"I'm not going away."

"Promise?"

"I promise. You're stuck with me."

It was the most wonderful thing anyone had ever said to her.

"You're so handsome and nice," she said. "I like your face. You've got such a big interesting nose, and I like a big nose on a man. I like having you around."

He let out a sort of surprised chuckle and shook his head.

"Well, I like being around you, too, Susana. And… I like your face, too. I like it a lot. And I'm not going anywhere. I'm staying right here for as long as you'll have me. Me and my big interesting nose."

FOR THE FIRST forty-eight hours, Susana had round-the-clock care. They split the days into three eight-hour shifts—Roque, Monika and Kristyna. Kristyna took the night shift and left early to work at the shop. Monika handled mornings through early afternoons. Roque took the midafternoons through the evenings.

He contacted all of Susana's students and told them that she was hurt and lessons would be rescheduled at a later time. It was easy to do because she kept such good records.

There wasn't a lot else for him to do at first. Susana was taking a lot of painkillers, and she mostly just slept. Roque knew it wasn't necessary to wake her every few hours like people used to do with head injuries; he remembered that from his own concussion, and it did make more sense to let her get plenty of uninterrupted sleep. But it worried him when she slept longer than an hour at a time. He wanted to go in and look at her and make sure she was breathing. He didn't do it, but he wanted to. And he always breathed a big sigh of relief once he heard her stirring in her room.

Then on the third evening, he woke from a nap on her sofa to find her staring at him.

She was standing there in her red plaid pajama pants and fleecy shirt, with her hair messed up and her arm in a child-sized sling.

It was raining, as it had been almost nonstop since the accident, and the sound of rain on a metal roof always made Roque sleepy. He blinked and stretched, waking Pirko, who was curled up at his feet. Technically Pirko wasn't allowed on the sofa, but all the upheaval had made her a worried little dog, and he'd figured she could use the comfort. It was a comfort to him, too.

"Hey," he said. "How do you feel?"

"Better," said Susana. "My head is clearer."

"Good. You hungry? We've got lots of good things to eat. Your mother brought over a bunch of pastries and taco stuff from the shop, plus some sort of noodle dish."

He knew she hadn't had much to eat so far. The nausea had been pretty bad.

"I'm not hungry, but I could go for a nice cup of tea," she said.

Roque got up and headed to the kitchen. "Coming right up."

He poured water into the electric kettle and started it heating, then took down two mugs and dropped tea bags into them.

"The horses are all fine," he said. "Oh, and you got four inches of rain today. I've been checking your rain gauge every day at evening feeding time. I got three and a half out at my place. You got four inches yesterday, too, and six inches before that. If this keeps up, the stock tanks are going to fill up."

She chuckled. "Are you actually talking about how much rainfall we've gotten?"

"Sure! I'm a fully naturalized Texan and we care about rain."

"Oh, I think you've been a fully naturalized Texan for a while now."

The water came to a boil. Roque poured it into the mugs and carried Susana's to the coffee table, along with a saucer and a spoon.

Susana was curled up in the spot he'd just vacated. Pirko lay on the sofa with her head resting on Susana's feet.

The coffee table was covered with

stacks of horse anatomy worksheets and registration forms.

"I found those papers lying around and stacked them up for you," Roque said as he went back for his own mug. "They're for horse camp, right? They look good. I've got some ideas for posters and things, and Jimmy Ray says we can put them up at the feed store."

Susana turned away. "You don't have to pretend you're going to be around for horse camp. I remember what happened. You're going to work for Dirk."

Roque set his mug down and sat on the sofa beside her. "Actually, I told Dirk that while I appreciate his offer, I have a prior commitment. I'm going to do what I can for him, and help at the ranch during roundups and calving season, but my top priority is here, with you."

She gave him a wary look. "You're not just saying that because I got hurt?"

"No. It's the truth. That's why I came back, to tell you I wasn't leaving. And to tell you that... I love you."

His heart pounded itself sore in his

chest. Susana just stared at him with those clear blue eyes.

"But working for Dirk was what you wanted," she said. "It was your dream."

"Dreams change," he said. "Besides, the part I always liked best about the ranch was the horses."

He swallowed hard. "When I got here and saw Leda all by herself with her saddle on, and you nowhere in sight, and Pirko running toward me, barking her head off... Well, I knew something was wrong. And when I found you on the trail and saw you lying there, my heart just about stopped. I thought I'd lost you for good."

She was quiet for a long time. His *I love you* hung in the air between them, unanswered.

"I shouldn't have made you choose," she said at last. "I should have trusted you more. But I'm glad you came back. And not just because I needed someone to take me to urgent care."

Then her eyes filled with tears. "I love you, too, Roque," she whispered.

And suddenly he was soaring. He tried

to speak, but couldn't get his voice to work right. He took a shaky breath and tried again.

"I'd really like to kiss you right now," he said, "but I'm afraid of hurting you."

"I'm willing to risk it," she said.

He leaned over, zeroing in so very slowly and carefully that she laughed at him. But laughing must have hurt her shoulder, because she said, "Ow." He started to back up then, but she reached out with her good hand and grabbed a fistful of his shirt.

"No," she said. "Don't go away. Kiss me."

Slowly and gently, he did.

It was achingly good to feel his lips against hers again, even if he was treating her like a delicate piece of glassware. She didn't mind that. He cupped her face in his hand and ran his thumb lightly over her cheekbone and stroked her hair with his fingertips.

He drew back, then kissed her on the forehead. "I'm glad you're feeling better," he said.

"Me too. Thank you for taking care of me."

"You kidding? No place I'd rather be. Oh, hey, I got us something to watch, once your head is ready for some screen time."

"What is it?"

He reached under the stack of papers and pulled out a DVD.

"*The Man from Snowy River*!" said Susana.

"Yeah, isn't that great? Macy had it at her house."

"Who's Macy?"

"Dirk's new neighbor and… Well, you'll see when you meet her. You want to watch it? You're past the time of having to be completely screen-free, but if your head still hurts—"

"I want to watch it," she said.

They settled in—Roque's back against the arm of the sofa, Susana's back against his chest, and Pirko at the sofa's other end, where she was apparently allowed to be now. Susana didn't mind. Roque drew the coffee table closer so they could reach their tea.

The movie was like an old friend. The soundtrack alone was enough to conjure up all her youthful longings. It was a part of the mountains, and the thundering hooves of the wild brumbies, and the jaw-dropping riding.

She felt safe and cocooned, with Roque's long slow breaths at her back and a blanket pulled over them both, the sound of rain on the metal roof and her favorite movie playing. When the other riders pulled up at the edge of the embankment, and Jim rode past them at a full gallop down the impossibly steep slope, and the horns played their heroic notes, she heard Roque let out a soft, "Whoa," and knew that he loved the movie as much as she did.

They watched all the way to the end of the credits to see the names of the stunt riders—all those Wallises and Egans and Purcells, entire families of superb Australian horsemen.

Susana was hungry now, so Roque made her some toast.

"You sure you don't want something else?" he asked. "We've got a fridge full of food here."

"Right now I just want toast, lightly buttered. It's my favorite comfort food."

The rain had stopped. Roque went out to do night check on the horses while Susana ate her toast. It was golden-crisp with exactly the right amount of butter, soaked in but not soggy—the best toast she'd ever had.

She had just finished when Roque came back inside, his face shining with joy.

"Do you feel well enough to come outside for a minute?" he asked. "Daisy had her foal."

CHAPTER TWENTY

DAISY'S FOAL WAS a pretty little filly, cream-colored all over, with blue eyes and a white mane and tail. The skin around her eyes was black, which meant she was a palomino like her mother and not a champagne. She was perfectly healthy. Susana called her Spindrift.

She started handling Spindrift right from the start so she'd be used to human contact. She rubbed, stroked and scratched the little foal from head to hoof, starting at the neck, back and chest and moving on to the head and legs, making it as pleasant an experience for her as possible so she'd have good associations with humans.

On the second day, Susana brought out a brush, a rag, a lead rope and a small halter for Spindrift to sniff and explore. By the time Spindrift was ten days old, she was so accustomed to the sight and smell of the halter that Susana was able to put it on her with no trouble at all. Soon after that, she was able to lead the foal with a cotton lead rope.

"She looks great," Roque said.

"She does, doesn't she? It's nice to have charge of a horse right from the start for a change, instead of having to undo the damage from other people's mistakes and mistreatment. The things she learns at this stage are foundational to all her future development. If I do it right, she'll be a pleasure to train and a pleasure to ride one day. She certainly has excellent conformation. She could sell for a good price one day, to the right buyer."

By now Susana didn't need constant care. She was getting around well enough, and her concussion symptoms had subsided to occasional slight headaches and mental fuzziness. Her mom and her sister still came over once a day or so, and Roque spent every evening with her. They watched *Return to Snowy River* and other horse movies and worked their way through the food Kristyna had brought.

One afternoon, Roque came over with

a bag of cheese curds from Lalo's and a DVD of *National Velvet*.

"I've got something to tell you," he said.

He looked so earnest and excited that Susana's heart skipped a beat. "Let's hear it," she said.

"I made a new deal."

"Ah. What is it this time? A new horse? A new student?"

"A new barn."

She turned and looked at him.

"Well, new to you," he said. "It's actually a very old barn, built in the late 1800s. But it turns out that's a good thing in barns, because back then they were made with virgin growth timber, which makes them more durable than newer barns, not to mention a whole lot better looking. The construction is post and beam, which means fewer parts, which is good, too. It's got a raised center aisle, a tack room and a feed room, and fourteen stalls, eight of which have runs. It doesn't have a wash station, but there's space to add one. And it's all yours."

Susana's head spun, and not from her concussion. It was too much to take in

"What—how—where did this barn come from? Did you find it on Craigslist or something?"

"No. I heard about it the other day at Lalo's. You know Don and Susan Hunter? They own that Architectural Treasures place in town that sells all that salvage stuff from old buildings that get demolished. They'd just come from an old ranch that's being sold to developers. The house is going to come down, and the Hunters are going to salvage what they can—you know, old doors and moldings and windows and such. There's a barn on the property, too. It's too much material for them to salvage—they've got so much inventory right now that they barely have enough space to store it, and anyway they do most of their business in smaller items. So I thought, why not take a look? So they gave me the contact info for the developers, and I called Zac, and he met me there. And the long and short of it is, we're going to take that barn apart and reassemble it here on your property."

It sounded too good to be true. "How good of shape is it in?"

"Fantastic. It's already been inspected for insects and moisture. I'm telling you, these old barns were built to last. And it's so *beautiful*, Susana. I wish you could see it. Actually, you can, because I took pictures."

He brought out his phone and showed her. She scrolled slowly through the images. The barn was gorgeous, all right. She could imagine it on her place, newly sided and roofed, clean and restful and shady, with contented horses in its roomy stalls, and a couple of dozen horse campers learning to pick feet and take care of tack under its roof.

"We'll have to check local codes for specifics about moving it and setting it up," Roque said. "And prep the site, and run the electrical, and fit out the plumbing. But once it's here, it should last the duration. Zac has already talked to a guy he knows, an older guy from Novak, a master carpenter, Jacob something."

"Jacob Geryk?"

"Yeah, that's it. He went out and looked at it, too. He's going to boss the job."

"Hold on," said Susana. "Before we

start lining up builders, I need to run some numbers. How much do the owners want for the barn?"

"Not a red cent. The land's already been sold, and the developers just want it off their property."

"Well, that's a good start. But it still won't be cheap. Transportation, labor, site preparation…"

"All taken care of. Mr. Mendoza has offered to do the dirt work and prep the pad for free. The Hunters have trucks that they use to haul materials to their shop, and they said they'll handle the transportation. And we've got a volunteer workforce all lined up—Zac and his crew, the church in Novak, Curt and some of his people, the Mendozas, the Ramirezes, the Reyeses, your clients and students, your neighbors, Dirk and his interns…"

Susana let out a shaky laugh. "How did you ever arrange all this?"

Roque shrugged. "Oh, you know, just asked around. I've been busy with it for a few days now. I wanted to have it all sorted out before mentioning any of it to you. The thing is, baby, people are happy to help you, because you do so much good yourself, rescuing horses and goats and dogs. You do so many good things that you forget to keep track of them. But other people don't forget."

She laughed again, louder this time. "I can't believe this. I don't know what to say."

He laid a hand against her cheek. "You're finally going to have it, baby. The barn of your dreams."

She took his hand in hers and kissed it. "And the man of my dreams."

CHAPTER TWENTY-ONE

THE EVENING BEFORE barn-raising day, Roque and Susana walked out to the prepped building site to take a look. The core crew of volunteer builders had completed as much of the work as possible ahead of time, taking the old barn apart, labeling all the pieces, moving them to Susana's place and arranging them exactly the way Mr. Geryk said to so they could be put back together in their original positions.

They'd finished building the foundation yesterday—Roque, Zac, the Reyes brothers, Roy Davidge, Mr. Mendoza and some of his sons. They'd laid the sills, joining the corners and squaring them up, then added the floor joists and girders, thwacking the joints into place with a big mallet called a commander, and constantly checking to make sure everything was level.

Next they'd put together the bents, pre-assembled cross sections that spanned the width of the frame. The four bents—one for each end and two in between—now lay flat on the temporary decking boards laid over the foundation timbers, ready to be raised into place tomorrow.

Roque crouched down and ran his fingers over a mortise and tenon joint in one of the bents. "Isn't it beautiful? No nails or screws, just old wood, specially shaped to fit together perfectly. All these pieces ready to do their part and come together to make something bigger."

Susana laid a hand on his back. "It's really happening, isn't it? After all the rain and the setbacks and the endless permits to file, it's finally coming together."

The barn-raising had been scheduled for mid-March, to coincide with spring break, but for a while it had looked as if the weather might derail the whole project. After several months with no rainfall whatsoever, Seguin County was suddenly getting a year's worth all at once.

But there'd been enough clear stretches between thunderstorms for the crews to do their work, and tomorrow's forecast called for clear skies.

"Of course it's coming together," said Roque. "I never had a moment's doubt."

He stood. Susana leaned against him, put her arm around his waist and hooked her fingers into his belt loop. "Thank you for doing this," she said. "I wish I could help with the actual work."

Roque kissed the top of her head. "You just let other people work for you for a change so that bone can heal. The sooner it does, the sooner you can get back to your real work with the horses. And when you do, you'll have an amazing barn to work out of. The barn of your dreams."

"Are you kidding? This is better than the barn of my dreams. I never aspired to dream this big. Never could have imagined when I bought this property that I'd one day see a nineteenth-century barn go up on the place."

"Yeah, it's pretty exciting. Mr. Geryk is having the time of his life."

As master builder, Mr. Geryk was in charge of the entire project. He'd already assigned work crews, each under the di-

rection of a crew chief who had experience with post and beam construction, and
made it clear what each crew was responsible for. He knew where every last timber
was supposed to go.

"I don't know how he keeps track of
it all," Roque went on. "It's like he's bal-
ancing all this information on the top of
his head. I keep thinking he's going to tip
over and it's all going to spill out. How old
is he, anyway? A hundred and twenty?"

Susana chuckled. "I don't know. As far
as I can remember, he's always looked exactly the same. He was part of the crew
that built the church building back in the
fifties, and Zac got his start in construction under him."

The volunteers started arriving before
dawn. Some people from Alex Reyes's
historical reenactment group showed up
wearing nineteenth-century attire and carrying old hand tools. Pirko was beside herself with joy to have so many visitors on
the place. The donated tacos and kolache
were set up on long tables near the house
along with big urns of coffee and plenty
of bottled water.

Roque gave Susana a kiss. "Good morning," he said. "You look beautiful."

"Thanks. Monika came over early to help with my hair and makeup. I told her it wasn't necessary, but she just said it's not every day that a girl gets a pre-1900 barn moved onto her property and half the town turns out to help put it together and that I had to look super cute for the occasion."

A piercing whistle cut through the crowd noise. "Hey, Fidalgo!" Zac called. "Stop messing around with my cousin and get over here. You're on my crew."

Roque kissed Susana again. "Gotta go."

The moment they'd all been waiting for came at last. It was time to raise the bents.

According to Mr. Geryk, it took one person for every fifty pounds of bent weight to be lifted. Roque didn't know how much each bent weighed, but it must have been a lot, because there were an awful lot of men lined up shoulder to shoulder, ready to hoist the bent. He had Johnny Mendoza on one side of him and Tony Reyes on the other. More men waited alongside for their turn.

Mr. Geryk's voice rang out in the morning. "Remember, everybody, lift from your legs. All right. Let's do it."

They took hold of the crossbeam and hefted it up.

A cheer rose up from somewhere. Once the bent plate reached chest height, some other guys dressed as frontiersmen, or defenders of the Alamo, or something, stepped in along the sides to shoulder the posts from lower down, moving them toward the vertical. Then pikemen came from behind, with long sharpened poles that bit into the wood to keep the upper bent steady. Slowly, they worked the posts upright.

At last, with a satisfying thud, the tenons dropped into place.

By nightfall, the walls were up and the massive summer beam had been set. There was plenty of carpentry left to be done, but the barn was well and truly raised.

EPILOGUE

THE SUN DIPPED low in the Texas sky, casting its last mellow light over dark green cedars, bronzy post oaks and elms still holding on to a light scattering of gold. Bright green vines clung to tree trunks in the understory. A rainy spring and summer had brought the drought to an official end. Now, near the close of December, the land looked rested and grateful.

Susana followed Roque along the Sweetheart Trail, her gaze focused on his broad back. In his black cowboy hat, with the skirts of his drover coat spread across the saddle, he could have been an old-time cowboy from a century and a half ago.

"You sure look good in that coat," she said.

He turned a little, showing her his strong profile. "Oh, yeah? As I recall, you didn't always think too highly of this coat."

"What? That isn't true. I always liked the coat. I just said it was kind of outlandish-looking and needed some honest wear. Both of which were true."

Roque chuckled. "Yeah, well, after a full year of working for you, I'd say it's got plenty of honest wear."

"It is a full year, you know," Susana said. "A year to the day since Cisco came ambling up my driveway and we officially met."

"Is it really? I didn't know that. We should have done something to celebrate."

Susana smiled. She knew something he didn't know.

"A sunset trail ride feels like celebration enough," she said.

"Yeah, that's true. Man, the place sure looks different, doesn't it?"

It did. Last year's snow and ice were a distant memory. There were more pens on the property now and a lot less brush. With the burn ban lifted, they'd even started to get rid of the brush piles from beside the trails, and also from the future hay field, which Roque had finished clearing only last week.

With all four trails completed by summer's end, they'd been giving a lot of trail rides. Visitors came from out of town to ride there, largely due to word-of-mouth recommendations, and Susana was thinking of building a little cabin on the property to use as an Airbnb. The therapeutic riding program was still just a possibility as of yet, but she and Roque had held their horse camp in June, and it had been so successful that they were planning a bigger one for next year, with two sessions for different age groups. All of which meant there was plenty of work to keep both of them busy full-time, and then some.

Speaking of which...

"Barrymore's owner called today," she said.

"Did he? I didn't think you ever heard from him."

"Hardly ever, though he always sends his payment on time, which is more than I can say for some folks. He's been boarding Barrymore here since I first started business, and he's never once come out to see him. He knows I've been using Barrymore as Gillian's lesson horse, and today he asked me if I thought she'd be interested in buying him."

"Well, how about that! How much is he asking?"

"Not as much as he could get from another buyer if he shopped him around. I don't think he really needs the money. I think he just wants to make sure Barrymore goes to a good home with someone who'll give him lots of attention. And he thinks Gillian is that person."

"Gillian doesn't have a place to keep a horse, though. She lives in town."

"Right. So I got to thinking, maybe I could alter my arrangement with her. At this point, she doesn't need riding instruction as much as she needs plenty of practice. She knows what to do—she just needs to do it. So what if I boarded Barrymore for her in exchange for twenty hours of work a week?"

Roque threw back his head and laughed. "Same deal you offered me! Perfect."

The trail ended where it had begun, at a split-rail fence with integrated mounting blocks and saddle trees that Roque and Susana had built together. The fence ran up against the barn and formed one side of the home pasture.

The barn stood solid and enduring in its tongue-and-groove siding and new metal roof. Spindrift was grazing in the home pasture. Her head lifted, her ears perked up and she let out a welcoming whinny to her mother. Daisy answered with a calm neigh. Spindrift was eight months old now, not yet at mature size, and still too young to saddle train, but Susana worked with her every day.

They dismounted, unsaddled and took care of the horses. The barn smelled of old wood and pine shavings, oil and leather, feed and horse. Mellow sunlight slanted in through the open windows.

About a month earlier, Susana's mother had suddenly said that the time had come to divvy up the family's supply of antique Bohemian glass bead jewelry among her daughters. She'd been talking about doing it for years—in fact, she'd dropped some heavy hints in front of Roque at the Chili Noodle Soup Supper—but this time, she took decisive action. All three sisters were assembled to go through the pieces, claim the ones they wanted and figure out a fair system of dividing them all.

Susana had found one ring she loved, with a cut-glass ruby-red crystal in a late Victorian gold filigree setting—her color, her style and it even fit her tiny hand. Monika had made an inventory of all the rings and who wanted what, then taken them all back to the safe-deposit box— or so she'd said. Susana had been certain that the red ring was going to Roque. He was going to propose! He'd set the whole ring thing up with Monika and her mother so he could present Susana with an heir-loom ring of her own choosing. What else could it mean?

Well, apparently it meant something else, because he hadn't proposed. Susana kept waiting and waiting, but as the days turned into weeks, she'd given up. She'd been a little disappointed at first, but too many good things were happening for her to stay down for long. Roque was here with her now, and that was enough.

Now he came up behind her, put his arms around her and rested his chin on the top of her head.

"So what do you want to do this weekend, boss?" he asked.

She smiled. "Actually, I thought we might get started on that entrance gate you keep bugging me to get."

Lately Roque had been all about entrance gates. Every time he drove anywhere, he seemed to see a new one. Then he had to tell Susana all about it—what it was made of, whether it had any landscaping around it, whether it was too plain or too gaudy or just right, and whether it was the sort of entrance gate that would look right at Susana's place.

He turned her around to face him. "Ooh, nice! Do you have any ideas about materials? It doesn't have to be all fancy with granite pillars and big wrought-iron archways. I've seen some really handsome ones with nothing more than chunks of limestone and big cedar posts. Just enough to set a tone, you know? First impressions are important."

"Limestone and cedar posts sounds good to me. They'd look good with the sign."

"What sign?"

"The entry sign I had made."

"I didn't know you had an entry sign made."

"Oh, didn't I mention it?"

"No. Where is it? I want to see it."

She took his hand and led him to the wall-mounted horse blanket rack. Meriadoc's blanket hung on the top rod. She swung it out of the way to reveal a black powder-coated steel sign hanging from the next rod down.

The design was simple and striking, easy to make out from a distance. It showed a logo of a stylized horse next to the words, Vrba-Fidalgo Equestrian Center.

Roque stood there a minute, staring. Then he reached out a hand and ran it along the letters of their two names. He looked from the sign to Susana and back again.

She saw him swallow hard.

"Does this… Do you…?" he began.

"I want to make you a partner," she said. "I've talked to a lawyer about the legal issues. There are some things to iron out.

but nothing we can't handle. So how about it? You want to be my business partner?"

He turned to face her. His eyes were shining.

"Yeah," he said. "Yeah, I do."

He took her in his arms and held her close for a long moment.

Then he let go and said, "Now I have a question for you."

He reached into his shirt pocket and pulled out—

It couldn't be a ring box. It couldn't! But when he opened it, a beam of light from the setting sun hit it, and Susana caught a flash of red.

Her hand flew to her mouth.

"I've been carrying this around with me for a while, trying to figure out the best time and place to ask," Roque said. "But nothing could be more perfect than this."

He pulled out the ring. It was even more beautiful than she remembered. Then he took her hand in his.

"So how about it?" he asked. "You want to marry me?"

She heard herself laughing. It was a

shaky, breathless sound, and there were tears on her cheeks, like rain in sunshine.

"I do," she said.

He grinned from ear to ear, like a happy-hearted boy.

He slid the ring onto her finger. The red stone glowed with a rich inner warmth all its own.

He took her in his arms and held her tight. She laid her cheek against his chest. Her tears soaked into the soft flannel of his shirt, and she could feel the beating of his heart, fast and strong.

* * * * *

Be sure to look for the next book in Kit Hawthorne's Truly Texas series available soon from Harlequin Heartwarming!